KT-497-934

MULBERRY GETS UP TO MISCHIEF

Che Golden

OXFORD
UNIVERSITY PRESS

OXFORD
UNIVERSITY PRESS

Great Clarendon Street, Oxford OX2 6DP

Oxford University Press is a department of the University of Oxford.
It furthers the University's objective of excellence in research, scholarship,
and education by publishing worldwide. Oxford is a registered trade mark of
Oxford University Press in the UK and in certain other countries

Text © Che Golden 2015
Cover and inside illustrations © Thomas Docherty 2015

The moral rights of the author, illustrator, and translator have been asserted

First published 2015

Database right Oxford University Press (maker)

All rights reserved. No part of this publication may be reproduced,
stored in a retrieval system, or transmitted, in any form or by any means,
without the prior permission in writing of Oxford University Press,
or as expressly permitted by law, or under terms agreed with the appropriate
reprographics rights organization. Enquiries concerning reproduction
outside the scope of the above should be sent to the Rights Department,
Oxford University Press, at the address above

You must not circulate this book in any other binding or cover
and you must impose this same condition on any acquirer

British Library Cataloguing in Publication Data
Data available

ISBN: 978-0-19-273472-3

1 3 5 7 9 10 8 6 4 2

Printed in Great Britain

Paper used in the production of this book is a natural,
recyclable product made from wood grown in sustainable forests.
The manufacturing process conforms to the environmental
regulations of the country of origin.

Kingston upon Thames Libraries	
KT 2185543 9	
Askews & Holts	29-Apr-2016
JF JF	£5.99
KN	KT00001405

The Meadow Vale Ponies

MULBERRY

GETS UP TO
MISCHIEF

KT 2185543 9

ALSO AVAILABLE:

Mulberry and the Summer Show

Mulberry for Sale

Mulberry to the Rescue!

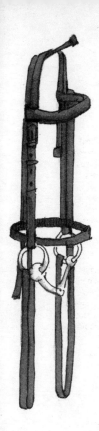

For Robbie,

the best cure

for a broken heart

Chapter 1

'One more jump. Just one more jump is all that stands between Samantha Grey and her champion mare, Mulberry, winning the showjumping competition for under 10s at this year's Horse of the Year Show. Can they do it? This pair has won every prize at Pony Club competitions up and down the country. Can they win this cup to become the most successful pony-and-rider combination ever?'

Sam flicked her heels against Mulberry's side and the little black mare leapt straight into canter. Dust from the arena surface puffed up beneath every beat of her neat blueish-black hoofs. Her long black mane flicked back against Sam's face as the two of them raced through the corner, Sam sitting back in the saddle and gently pulling on one rein to steady Mulberry. She didn't want the little mare losing her balance by taking a corner too quickly. Sam turned her head to look at the jump, steering Mulberry towards it as they both curved away from the arena wall and thundered in a straight line towards the raised poles. Mulberry tucked her head down and put on a burst of speed, Sam no longer able to hold her back in her excitement. Sam swallowed as the jump rushed towards them, looming large. It was bigger than anything they had ever jumped before. Could they make it? Or were they going to end up on the floor in a tangle of limbs?

Although Sam's confidence was wavering, it was too late. Mulberry tensed her muscles and leapt over the jump. Sam stood up in her stirrups and pushed the reins up Mulberry's neck so she wouldn't catch the little mare in

the mouth with the metal bit. She closed her
eyes as Mulberry came down in a steep dive
over the straight poles and leaned back as
far as she could over Mulberry's broad back

in an effort to stop herself flipping over the mare's neck and onto the ground.

Sam felt the jolt as Mulberry's front hoofs found the arena surface again and she quickly sat up as they galloped away from the jump. She leaned back again and tugged on the reins, slowing Mulberry to a stop. Sam jumped down from the saddle and leapt about, whooping with delight.

'They did, they did it! Sam Grey and Mulberry have WON the under 10s show-jumping competition at HOYS! The crowd goes wild with applause!'

A little dun-coloured Shetland pony with a wild, bushy mane poked her nose over the top of the arena wall. 'Well, they would do, if there was anyone here. And if you were actually at HOYS,' said Apricot.

Sam looked over at the little mare and sighed. It was a special gift, being able to talk to animals, but sometimes it was a pain being able to hear what they said. 'Could you not just let me dream for a little while?'

'Dreaming? Pure idiocy if you ask me,' snorted Apricot.

'Well, no one did ask you, so shut it,' said Mulberry. Apricot ducked her head back down and carried on munching at a hay net that had been tied up for her, but Sam could still hear her complaining.

Mulberry nuzzled Sam with her soft nose. 'You are daft, though,' she said. 'This isn't HOYS and there's no one here.'

Sam sighed. Ponies didn't have much imagination and had very little time for day-dreaming. 'I know that,' she said. 'I'm just pretending, remember?'

'Pretending—that's when you tell yourself whopping lies, isn't it?' asked Mulberry. 'Because it's . . . fun?'

Sam nodded.

'I still don't get it,' Mulberry sighed. 'But

whatever makes you happy.'

Sam grinned and threw her arms around Mulberry's neck to give her a big hug.

'It was the biggest jump we've ever done,' said Mulberry, nuzzling Sam with her soft nose. 'If we were at HOYS we would be doing a victory lap right now, wouldn't we?'

'We would!' squealed Sam. 'NOW you're getting the hang of daydreaming!'

'I'm not,' said Mulberry, giving her a big lick on the cheek. 'I still think you're daft, but if we are going to do this, we might as well do it right. Hop back on and let's get this over with. I'm hungry.'

Giggling, Sam put a foot in the stirrup and swung her leg over Mulberry's back. No sooner was she in the saddle than the little mare took off at a gallop, whizzing round and round the arena while Sam smiled and waved at the imaginary, cheering crowd.

After a couple of minutes they slowed down again and Sam gave Mulberry a long rein and let her walk around the arena so she could cool down properly. The weather was getting cold and she didn't want Mulberry to get a chill. Ponies could get sick if you simply let them stand in the cold with sweaty coats. As they dawdled round, Amy, Sam's big sister, came running down to the arena, breathless with excitement.

'I think I've found him,' she called to Sam, a huge smile splitting her face in two. 'I think I've found the perfect pony! Come into the

office and look at his ad on the internet!'

'Let me just put Mulberry back into her stable . . .' said Sam.

'Oh, we'll only be five minutes!' said Amy. 'Just tie her up by the wall and chuck a fleece on her—she'll be fine.'

Sam didn't like to say no to Amy so she got down and led Mulberry out of the arena. A lot of the riding-school ponies were being used today for a birthday party so there were plenty of head collars and lead ropes tied to brass rings screwed to the arena wall. She tied a head collar around Mulberry's neck, slipped the bridle off her head gently, and then tied the head collar around Mulberry's face, so that the mare would be comfortable and safe. It wasn't a good idea to tie a pony up by the bridle—if they panicked over something and fought to get loose, they could hurt their mouths very badly. Not that Sam could imagine Mulberry panicking.

Normally everyone on the yard made an effort to stay out of her way, but still, Sam thought it best to be safe. She grabbed a spare fleece lying over an empty stable door and threw it on Mulberry's back to keep her nice and warm.

'I'll be five minutes and then I'll spoil you rotten,' Sam whispered in Mulberry's ear as she gave her a kiss on the cheek. 'Promise.' And with that she ran quickly into the office.

'And so it starts,' said Apricot, her eyes gleaming.

'No, it doesn't,' said Mulberry, through gritted teeth.

'What starts?' said a squeaky little voice as two ferrets came loping around the corner.

'Nothing that's got anything to do with you weasels,' said Mulberry, leaning down and blowing hard through her wide nostrils. The ferrets screwed their eyes shut and stood their ground in the blast, even though their

thick fur was blown back from their faces.

'So what is starting?' said the bigger, black and cream male called Mike. 'A barbeque?'

'Do you ever think about anything else but food?' asked Mulberry.

'Do you?' he asked.

'Touché,' said Mindy.

Apricot cleared her throat. 'AS I WAS SAYING.' She paused and made sure they were all looking at her, although Mulberry was really glaring. 'It's started.'

Mindy sighed. 'What has, clever clogs? Spit it out!'

'Mulberry isn't going to be the only pony in the family any more,' said Apricot. 'Maybe Sam won't be bothered about riding her from now on.'

'We have loads of fun. She's not going to give up riding me,' snapped Mulberry.

'Sez you!' sneered Apricot.

Mike rolled over onto his back and

scratched at his belly, yawning. 'You've lost me,' he muttered. 'I have no idea what any of you are on about.'

'You've got about two seconds to grab his attention or he's going to fall asleep,' warned Mindy.

'Well, it's simple,' said Apricot, a smug look on her face. 'Sam's family are getting a new pony, and I bet it's young and flashy. Sam will want to ride the new pony and, eventually, Mulberry will be forgotten about.'

'Sam wouldn't do that!' said Mike.

'Why, because she's the only two-legs we know that can talk to animals?' said Apricot. 'She's still just a little girl. And little girls grow up and forget their old pets.'

'You KNOW Sam isn't like that,' said Mulberry.

Apricot snorted. 'You know how it normally goes, Mulberry, so don't kid yourself. It's the older rider that gets the pony first and then it gets handed down to the little sister. Amy should have been the one to get a pony, not Sam. They only persuaded their mother to buy you because they felt sorry for you. You were a mistake. When the new pony comes along, who is going to want to bother with the cheap pony no one wanted to buy?'

Mulberry lunged forward and snapped her teeth at Apricot, the ferrets squealing and scurrying out of the way. Apricot stepped back and the rope stopped Mulberry short.

'There is NOTHING cheap about me,' said Mulberry. 'And Sam's MY girl!'

'YOUR girl? That's the problem when you spend all your time hanging around with one rider—you forget that they've got a lot of distractions,' said Apricot.

'What do you mean?' asked Mulberry.

Apricot looked innocent and shrugged. 'Nothing. Just that Sam's got her family and all her friends at school and now there's going to be another pony in the family. You're not the centre of her world, the way she is to you.'

Mulberry turned away and stamped her feet. Apricot was just trying to be annoying. Sam would never forget about her. Would she?

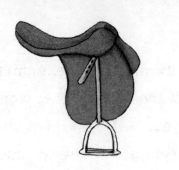

Chapter 2

Mulberry was in a very bad mood. She didn't have a watch and she couldn't tell the time, but she was sure Sam had been a lot longer than five minutes. Mulberry didn't like to be kept waiting. Sam knew this and so Mulberry decided she wasn't going to speak to her as punishment. So when Sam led her back to her stable, she jammed her head against the back wall and refused to look round at Sam, no matter how hard Sam tried to coax her over to the door. In fact, Mulberry was downright furious because Sam had a juicy, tart, green apple in her pocket, Mulberry's favourite, and she was too angry to come over even for *that*.

She had a point to make. She kept her big bottom facing Sam and her thick, glossy black tail swished from side to side, just like a cat in a temper.

Sam sighed. 'Can we at least talk about this?'

'There is *clearly* nothing to talk about,' said Mulberry to the wall. 'Because it's all done now, isn't it? And no one bothered to ask my opinion when you were all making your minds up about it, so no one is going to listen to me now, are they?'

'You're taking this the wrong way,' said Sam.

'I am not!' said Mulberry. 'There is only one way to take this whole fiasco and I am taking it. Don't complain that you don't like the way I am reacting; you have no one to blame but yourself. And perhaps that silly sister of yours.'

'Mulberry, please, it's not going to make any difference,' said Sam. But Mulberry carried on sulking and her tail carried on swishing.

'What's up with Her Maj?' asked a little voice by Sam's foot. She looked down to see Mindy blinking up at her. Mike loped up to Sam with his funny, hopping run and leaned against her riding boot, yawning in the crisp winter sunshine.

'Um, she's a little bit upset . . .' said Sam. Mindy dug her claws into Sam's boots and scrambled up her body, her sharp claws pricking Sam's skin through her clothes. She scrambled onto Sam's shoulder and then leapt onto the narrow edge of the stable door, her bottlebrush of a tail whipping from side to side as she fought for her balance. As soon as Mindy had stopped rocking on her perch, she cocked her narrow head at Mulberry.

'Oi,' she squeaked. 'Why the long face?'

Mike sniggered. 'Good one.'

'Could you get rid of the weasles, Sam?' Mulberry asked the wall in a voice that positively dripped with disdain. 'I don't want them stinking up my stable.'

'Ferrets,' said Mindy coolly. 'And there is no need to get snotty. You wouldn't like it if I called you a thoroughbred now, would you?'

'You'd have to be blind to mistake her for a thoroughbred,' snorted Mike.

Sam cringed as the ferrets squealed with laughter, their wicked white fangs flashing in the sun.

'I'd be offended, if you two didn't look like pot-bellied snakes,' said Mulberry.

'Ooh,' said both the ferrets at the same time. 'Cheek!'

'What *is* wrong with her?' Mindy asked Sam. 'Not that I care or anything—I am merely idly curious.'

Mulberry snorted. 'Idle is the right word.'

'She's feeling a bit put out because, well . . .' Sam stuttered, her face going red as Mulberry's tail swished faster.

'Yeeees?' wheedled Mindy.

'Well, we, that is, Amy, is—' Sam dropped her voice to a whisper. 'Amy is getting a new pony.'

Mulberry shook her head and made a harrumphing noise that echoed around the stable.

'Oh, that, we all heard about *that*,' said Mindy. '*She* said it was no big deal—but it seems there's a bit of the green-eyed monster going on, isn't there?'

'I am not jealous,' said Mulberry.

'Nah, 'course you're not, twinkle toes,' sniggered Mindy.

Sam heard a familiar whistling snore and looked down to see Mike draped over her boot, his long body snaking away onto the concrete floor of the yard. He was fast asleep.

'How does he do it?' she asked Mindy. 'He falls asleep anywhere, if you just let him be still for long enough.'

Mindy looked down at her brother and shrugged her shoulders. 'It's a talent,' she said. She looked back at Mulberry. 'If you're just going to sulk, I'm off.'

'Don't let me keep you,' huffed Mulberry. 'I'm sure

there is a rat somewhere you could bore to death.'

'No rats round here any more,' said Mindy as she leapt back onto Sam's shoulder and began to climb her way down. 'I can do my job.'

It was true—the rats that had been cheeky enough to sneak onto the yard looking for scraps of spilt hard feed had learned to avoid Meadow Vale as soon as the ferrets moved in. It was lucky for the brother and sister that the yard had decided to adopt them. Food and water was always left next to the quiet corner of the barn where they had made their home and they were well fed, sleek, and glossy.

Mindy sighed as she looked down at her brother, then she ran round to his tail, sank her teeth into it, and gave it a hard yank. Mike's eyes flew open and he gave a squeak as he slid off Sam's boot.

He looked at Mindy accusingly.

'Why are you biting my tail? You'll wreck my fur,' he complained.

'Because I'm tired of biting your smelly bum,' she snapped. 'Come on, its lunchtime and then I want a nap.'

Sam sighed as the ferrets loped off, bickering as they went.

'This is silly, Mulberry,' she said. 'Amy is the one getting the pony. Not me.'

'It doesn't matter,' said Mulberry. 'This family doesn't need a new pony. You've got me and Velvet. That's enough.'

'Mulberry, Velvet is bonded with Mum and you and I are bonded together,' said Sam. 'You can understand Amy feeling a bit left out and wanting a pony of her own.'

Mulberry just snorted and her tail swished from side to side like the executive toy Sam's father had sitting on his desk: little balls that clicked from side to side in constant motion, something Mulberry would do if she wound herself up enough.

'This has got nothing to do with you and me, Mulberry, nothing at all,' said Sam. 'I'm not going to be riding this new pony or looking after it. That's Amy's job.'

Mulberry looked over her shoulder at Sam, her black eyes narrowed with suspicion.

'You promise?' she asked.

'Mulberry, I won't even look at this pony, cross my heart and hope to die,' said Sam.

'Stick a needle in your eye if you tell a lie?' asked Mulberry.

Sam nodded.

'Do you know what a needle is and where I can get one?' asked Mulberry.

Sam reached into her pocket and pulled out the apple. 'Why don't you come over here, eat this apple, and let me give you a cuddle?'

'I suppose I could,' said Mulberry, turning

around and sidling over to the door. She stretched her neck out, her lips reaching out for the apple.

'Friends again?' asked Sam as she slid a hand beneath Mulberry's long thick mane and stroked her silky neck.

''Spose,' said Mulberry, her mouth full of apple.

'Do you fancy going for a hack tomorrow?' asked Sam as she scratched Mulberry behind the ears. The little mare half closed her eyes with contentment as she munched on the apple.

'I could do with a canter, out in the fresh air,' said Mulberry. 'Somewhere there are no Shetlands or ferrets.'

Sam laughed. 'Peace and quiet!'

Mulberry pricked her ears up and looked at Sam eagerly. 'Could we go on the golf course this time and have a gallop in that lovely, thick, springy grass?'

'We're not allowed on the golf course, Mulberry, I keep telling you that.'

'All that time and effort they spend on making that grass so nice to run on,' grumbled Mulberry. 'It's wasted on two-legs who don't go faster than a walk.'

Sam tried to hide a smile as she thought about what her golf-loving father would have to say about *that*, while Mulberry nuzzled her, hoping for another apple.

'Never mind,' she said as she patted the mare's glossy neck. 'We can still have fun in the woods.'

Chapter 3

Amy, Sam's big sister, longed for her own pony, like most pony-mad girls. She had spent years learning to ride and helping Mum with her own horse, a beautiful Irish cob mare called Velvet. Amy knew she would never be able to earn enough money to buy a pony as well trained as Velvet—animals like that were very expensive. She knew that her first pony would have to be young and inexperienced, so she had to work hard to prove to Mum and her instructor that she was sensible enough, and a good enough rider, to be able to handle a young pony and give it a good start in life. Mum had drummed into Amy over and over again that a young horse got its education and all its habits, good and bad, from its first rider. Amy had to be sure she could teach it all the right things. She had also got a Saturday job and worked at the yard, until, with some money from Mum and Dad and Christmas and birthday money from the whole family, she finally had enough for a pony of her own.

Sam had had great fun helping Amy shop for her pony. They had bought magazines and curled up on the sofa, poring over the adverts, and had spent hours clicking through ads online. Amy had thought carefully about what she wanted. She had decided on a native pony, just like Velvet and Mulberry. But it had to a big pony, capable of carrying an adult, because Amy was thirteen now and she didn't want to have to sell the pony on if she outgrew it. She had looked through lots of horse books and had gone to lots of shows until she had settled on the breed she wanted; a Scottish Highland pony, the biggest of the native breeds.

So that was how they had ended up driving to a stud in the heart of the countryside, as the few remaining red and gold leaves fluttered on the branches. Amy had done her research and picked a stud that produced sweet-natured ponies. Luckily, it had a gelding for a sale, who had been trained to wear a saddle and have a rider on his back that year, so Amy would be able to ride him straight away.

Sam knew Amy had fallen in love as soon as the lady who ran the stud, Dawn, brought them down to the stables.

'This is Robbie,' she said. 'He is an absolute sweetie.'

The pony who popped his head over the stable door was one of the most gorgeous creatures Sam had ever seen (apart from Mulberry, of course). He was broad-chested and muscular, with caramel dapples all over his body. He had a creamy mane that fell to his knees and the biggest, darkest doe eyes. He stretched his creamy face over the door and snuffled at Amy's face with his nostrils flared wide.

'Oh,' breathed Amy, her face flushing pink and two stars lighting up in her eyes.

'He's beautiful!'

Dawn smiled. 'He certainly is.'

Sam, Mum, and Dad gathered around Amy to pet Robbie, and the young pony wriggled with delight, enjoying being the centre of attention. He snuffled and snuggled his head into them and he closed his eyes and nickered with pleasure when Amy scratched him behind his ears.

He also nipped!

'Ouch!' said Mum, rubbing her arm where a red welt in the shape of Robbie's teeth was coming up.

'That is something you have to watch out for with young ponies,' said Dawn cheerfully. 'They do have a tendency to bite.' Dad gave a strangled yelp as Robbie took his sunglasses off his head and began to chew on them thoughtfully. 'And put everything in reach in their mouths. But don't worry, he'll soon grow out of it,' said

Dawn as Amy fished inside Robbie's mouth with her fingers and removed the now very wet shades.

Dawn turned to Amy. 'Would you like to tack him up and see how you get on in the saddle?' Amy nodded eagerly.

While Robbie may have looked the dream pony in the stable, Sam was disappointed to watch Amy ride him. She was so used to her amazing big sister jumping high and fast or cantering figures of eight in the arena that it was very odd to watch Amy barely get Robbie into a trot.

'This feels really weird,' Amy admitted to Dawn, who was watching her from the fence.

'I'm afraid riding a youngster like this is going to be nothing at all like riding an experienced horse,' said Dawn. 'He really only knows how to walk, trot, and canter in a straight line at this stage. Working in the arena will be very hard on him until he is fitter and better balanced with your weight on his back. He won't find it easy to bend through the corners, and cantering through them will be hard for a long time. It is down to you to teach him all this and to make sure he finds learning fun. Do you still think you want to do it?'

Amy chewed her lip. 'Do *you* think I will be able to?' she asked Dawn.

'I think that with plenty of help from your mother and your instructor, you and Robbie should get along just fine,' she said. 'Highlands are clever and quick to learn, but they are also docile and gentle. I don't think he will give you too much trouble.'

Amy smiled and patted Robbie on the neck. 'Then yes, please, I really want to own him.'

Dawn beamed at her. 'That's wonderful! Why don't you untack and groom him while your parents and I have a chat?'

Amy dismounted and began to walk Robbie from the arena. The young pony surprised her by giving a huge yawn and he blinked at her sleepily while everyone laughed.

'That's another thing you're going to have to get used to—young ponies get tired very quickly,' said Dawn. 'Fifteen minutes of work and the big lump is ready for a nap!'

'Could I go down to that field and pet those ponies?' asked Sam, pointing to a lush field in front of the main house. Amy shot her a grateful smile. Sam had guessed her sister would want to spend a little bit of time with her new pony on her own.

'Only if it is OK with Dawn,' said Dad.

Dawn waved Sam away. 'That's perfectly all right, but don't go into the field without an adult. Those youngsters can be very playful and they don't realize how big they are.'

'And stay in sight of the house,' Mum called after her as Sam ran down to the field.

'I will!' Sam called back over her shoulder.

The stud was a beautiful place. It was in the middle of nowhere and set well back from the main road so Sam couldn't even hear the sound of a car, just birdsong and the last few leaves in the trees rustling as the cold breeze ruffled them. The autumn sky was a pale blue, full of clouds being chased by the cold wind. Highland ponies dotted the fields around her. Some were filled with youngsters while others had mares grazing with frisky foals skipping around them. The field she was walking down to had six young ponies munching away in it.

Sam leaned against the fence and smiled

at a little mare who stopped grazing to look
at her curiously.

'Hello,' said Sam. 'What's your name?'

'I haven't got one yet,' said the little filly.

'Of course not, silly me,' said Sam.

'You can hear me?' asked the mare, while
five more heads popped up and gazed at

Sam. Sam nodded shyly as the youngsters
began to walk over to her.

'Are you the family who have come to
see Robbie?' one pony asked. Sam nodded.
'Are you going to take him away?' asked
another anxiously.

'My sister really likes him so, yes, it does

look as if he is coming home with us,' said Sam.

'Will you be nice to him?' asked the little mare.

'Of course we will!' said Sam.

'Is everyone nice to the ponies that leave here?'

Oh dear. Sam thought about that for a second. You heard stories of people who didn't care properly for their horses, who let them go hungry or hit them when they were angry. But no one she knew did anything like that. She didn't want to lie, but she didn't want to scare these baby ponies either. She took a deep breath.

'No one I know has ever been horrible to their ponies,' she said. 'I don't think Dawn would let you go anywhere she thought was not a good home either. She asked us lots and lots of questions before we came out here. We kind of had to prove we were nice people before she would even let us see Robbie.'

The youngsters looked at each other and nodded their heads. 'That's true,' they all said. 'Dawn loves us. She always gives us a kiss when she comes to check on us.'

'Robbie's been learning lots of new things,' said the little mare. 'I start my training next year, Dawn says. So I'll be going to a new home soon as well.'

One little filly shook her mane. 'I don't want to leave the stud,' she said in a small, frightened voice. 'I don't want to go to a strange place, full of strange two-legs. I don't want to be in a stable on my own like Robbie is during the day.'

'But when a family buys you, you have special people all of your own who will love you and kiss you and groom you every single day,' said Sam.

'I will?' asked the little filly, her face brightening.

Sam nodded. 'You will get to bond with a rider of your own and nothing is more amazing than that.'

'Sam!'

Sam looked over her shoulder and saw her mum waving to her.

'I have to go,' she said. 'Don't worry, you're all going to have wonderful homes.'

She ran back up to the main house as the youngsters whinnied a goodbye. She was so happy for Amy, and so pleased Robbie was going to be part of their family.

Chapter 4

It was the day Robbie was due to arrive. Amy was positively bouncing with excitement and Sam couldn't get a sensible word out of her all morning. She decided to take Mulberry out for a ride instead and let Amy get on with getting Robbie's stable ready. Amy was going to want to show Robbie off when he arrived and there would be lots of oohing and aahing as everyone admired him. Sam figured it was going to take a long time for her sister to come down off cloud nine. She knew how she had felt when she finally got to call herself Mulberry's owner. She hadn't heard a thing anyone had said to her, didn't remember eating anything, and had spent hours just staring at Mulberry in the stable and the field, telling herself over and over again that the beautiful black pony she was staring at was really hers until the mare told her all the attention was getting embarrassing. But from the way Mulberry had preened and pranced past the Shetlands with her nose in the air, Sam knew she had loved every minute of it.

But now Mulberry was grumpy and distant, not at all her usual self on a hack. Normally, Mulberry loved going for a ride in the countryside, especially when it was just the two of them. But she didn't take any interest in the sights and sounds around them and only grunted when Sam tried to talk to her.

Mulberry had obviously picked up on the excitement on the yard and was feeling a bit left out. When they got back to their stable,

Mulberry nudged Sam in the small of her back with her soft nose.

'I want some attention,' she said.

'What do you think I've been doing all morning?' asked Sam.

'That's work,' said Mulberry. 'I want a bit of spoiling.'

Sam sighed and scratched the little mare behind the ears. 'You're all hot and sweaty. How about I give you a bath and then you can go out into the field for a roll in the grass?'

Mulberry gave Sam a nudge with her nose. 'Lovely!'

Sam untacked Mulberry and tied her up while she went to fetch a bucket, some shampoo, and sponges. She ran some

warm water into the bucket and put a small squirt of Mulberry's favourite mint-smelling shampoo into it. She swirled her hand around in the water to make it foam. Mulberry sniffed the air with delight as Sam walked towards her, leaning to one side with the heavy bucket.

'Menthol Head and Shoulders!' she squealed. She sniffed at the bucket as Sam put it down on the floor. 'Put some more in. I want to have lots of bubbles.'

'No, Mulberry, you know that's not a good idea,' warned Sam as she dunked the sponge in the water and began to wash Mulberry's sweaty coat.

'Let's live dangerously and add another squirt,' said Mulberry.

Sam shook her head. 'Your skin is too sensitive for lots of human shampoo, Mulberry. I have explained this. Remember that time you dunked a whole bottle of

L'Oréal shampoo in your bucket when I wasn't looking?'

'I thought I was worth it,' said Mulberry.

'Yes, well, Mum and Dad didn't think so when they got the vet's bill for a tetanus jab and stitches after you tore your skin rubbing yourself against barbed wire.'

'It was the only thing that stopped the itching,' complained Mulberry.

'What, tearing your skin?' asked Sam. 'And you are asking me to let you do it again? No chance!' She started to rub the sponge on Mulberry's neck in big circles, the diluted shampoo foaming in fizzy bubbles. 'How does that feel?'

Mulberry thought about it for a second. 'Tingly,' she purred, wriggling with pleasure.

'There you go,' said Sam. 'It doesn't need to be any stronger.'

Mulberry sighed happily as Sam soaped her body down and rinsed all the shampoo

off with clean water. She tried to step back out of the way, but as usual, Mulberry was too quick, shaking her whole body hard so that Sam was soaked from head to foot.

'Don't forget the conditioner,' said Mulberry. 'I don't want my hair to be dry and unmanageable.'

Sam waved the bottle of mane and tail conditioner at her. 'Do I ever forget, Your Majesty?' She sprayed it on, combing it through Mulberry's tangled mane with her fingers. It was good stuff. Horse hair was thick and tough, but the conditioner made manes and tails soft and silky and repelled mud and water. Sam had tried it on her own hair once, but it had made it greasy and limp and it had taken Mum ages to wash it all out. She hadn't been amused when Sam had pointed out that at least she was waterproof and wouldn't need an umbrella for the next few days.

Finally, a tired, damp, and dirty Sam

stepped back to admire her handiwork. Mulberry gleamed like a polished gem in the sunshine and her mane and tail rippled like water. Mulberry preened. 'I'll say it if you don't,' she said. 'I am *so* good-looking, it hurts. Now throw a fleece over me before I freeze.'

Just then, Amy came bustling onto the lower yard, a big, happy smile on her face. Her cheeks were pink and her eyes sparkled as she threw her arms around Sam and gave

her a big squeeze. 'He's arrived!' she said. 'And he is even more gorgeous than I remember. Why don't you bring Mulberry over and we'll see how they get on?'

'Where is he?' asked Sam.

Amy let go of Sam and stepped back. 'Wow, you really smell of pony,' she said. 'I turned him out in the same field as Velvet. Let Mulberry go out as well and they can get used to each other.'

'Um, in a minute,' said Sam. 'I just have to tidy up here.'

Amy looked disappointed. 'OK. I'll go down to the field later and see how they are doing.'

Sam bent down and began to pick up her stuff as Amy walked away. She looked at Mulberry. 'What do you think?'

The little black mare shrugged. 'I suppose we might as well get this over and done with. I have to meet him sooner or later.'

'Good girl,' said Sam.

Chapter 5

Velvet, Mum's big, jet black Irish cob, had clearly decided to look after Robbie. When Sam and Mulberry got to the field, Robbie was clinging to her side, nuzzling her shoulder and staring with his big dark eyes at the curious Shetlands, who had gathered around for a good look at the new arrival.

'He's just a big version of us, isn't he?' Sam heard Turbo asking as she and Mulberry walked over.

'Well, his legs aren't six inches long and his belly doesn't touch the ground when he is standing up, but, yes, he's just like you,' said Velvet.

'We're all Scots here,' said Mickey. 'We should stick together, young 'un.'

'Yes, you'd be better off hanging out with us— we've more in common with you,' said Turbo.

'You were all born in Somerset,' said Velvet to the Shetlands. 'You're about as Scottish as I am!'

Turbo frowned. 'Is Somerset not in Scotland then?'

'NO!' everyone shouted at the same time.

'Anyway, I decide who gets to join our gang,' said Apricot, stamping her tiny little hoof and shaking her mane. 'And I'm not sure I want a big baby hanging around with us.' She narrowed her eyes at Robbie who pressed tighter to Velvet's side and gazed at Apricot with his big eyes. 'Babies are nothing but trouble.'

'That's not true,' said Robbie. 'I'm a good boy. Dawn said so!'

The rest of the Shetlands giggled while Apricot stared at Robbie, outraged at being answered back.

'Are you giving me lip, young 'un?' she asked.

Robbie looked confused. 'I don't think so. I don't think I can take my lips off.'

'See? This is why they are trouble!' declared Apricot to no one in particular. 'Babies don't know anything!'

'I know lots!' said Robbie, arching his neck and looking pleased with himself. 'I can walk, trot, and canter with a saddle and rider on my back now.'

'Really?' asked Apricot. 'What do you do when you see a car then?'

Again, Robbie looked confused and shot a look at Velvet. 'What's a car?'

'See!' said Apricot. 'That's a basic thing for a pony to know, that is. Not. A. Clue.'

Velvet shook her head in disgust at Apricot while Sam sighed. 'He will learn, Apricot. We all have to start somewhere,' said Sam.

'Well, I'm not teaching him,' said Apricot. 'It's boring!'

'Who asked you to?' asked Velvet. 'Typical Shetland, always complaining about something!'

Apricot stamped her little hoofs.'Don't think you can insult me, just 'cause you're big.'

She looked so fierce as she marched forward that Robbie took a step back without thinking and backed his bum right into the electric fence that was humming away behind him. He squealed with surprise as the electricity zapped him and he jumped forward while the Shetlands and Mulberry rolled around on the grass, laughing.

'What was *that*?' he asked as he looked at

the fence and then at his tail, his eyes wide with amazement.

'Oh, stop laughing,' said Velvet. 'He's probably never seen an electric fence before in his life. He's got so much to learn about the world and about being on a yard. You were the same yourself once.'

'I was never!' said Apricot, outraged.

'How sad that you have completely forgotten what it is like to be young,' said Velvet. 'What a miserable existence you must lead if you can't get in touch with your inner foal.'

Sam thought Apricot and her inner foal were doing just fine when Apricot stuck her tongue out at Velvet and blew a raspberry.

'Don't worry about it, young 'un,' said Turbo. 'We Scottish ponies are tough. Once you get used to the shock, an electric fence isn't that bad. Watch!'

Before anyone could stop him, Turbo charged straight at the fence, chest puffed

out, and squealed as the shock made him jump about three feet in the air.

'See?' he panted, swaying a little on his hoofs. 'No bother at all.'

'You do realize you're destroying brain cells every time you do that?' Apricot asked him. 'In your case, that explains a lot.'

'Is anyone else smelling burning hair?'

asked Mickey as he sniffed the air. 'No? Just me then.'

Turbo ignored them all. 'It's even better in the winter,' he explained to a wide-eyed Robbie. 'We tough little natives grow such thick winter coats, we hardly even feel the zap, as long as you go through the fence chest first. That didn't hurt at all.'

'That's true,' said Mickey. 'Grow a thick enough coat and you can field-hop all over the place.'

'What's field-hopping?' asked Robbie.

'That's enough of that,' snapped Velvet. 'I am NOT allowing you lot to teach him to field-hop or to give him any other bad habits.'

'There's no fun having a baby on the yard if we can't corrupt him,' said Apricot.

'It's not about you having fun,' said Velvet. She looked at Robbie. 'If you want to settle into this family and have a home for life, you must be a pony that brings joy and fun to your rider. If you start breaking fences and roaming from field to field, you will be thrown off the yard. That will NOT make Amy or her mother happy, I assure you.'

'I am a good boy,' said Robbie, looking up at Velvet from beneath his long, creamy forelock. 'I want to make Amy happy.'

'I know you are a good boy,' said Velvet in her warm, gentle voice. 'These silly ponies are just teasing you. Listen to me, pay attention: try your hardest to learn and you will fit in very well in our family.'

'I wouldn't rule out the field-hopping completely, though,' said Mulberry. 'If you get fed up of living here, there's always the open road and a life of freedom.' Sam dug her elbow into Mulberry's ribs. 'What?' Mulberry asked.

'Stop teasing him or I'll give you a life of freedom,' she warned. She smiled at Robbie, who looked so timid, snuggled tight against Velvet's side. She longed to pat him and reassure him, but she didn't want to make Mulberry jealous. 'You'll do just fine, Robbie, I know it. And Amy loves you already.'

The little pony's face brightened. 'Does she?'

'She does,' said Sam. 'She's going to be your special person, you wait and see.'

'Just like Sam is mine,' said Mulberry.

Sam patted her on the shoulder. 'Easy, tiger.'

Chapter 6

Over the next few days, Sam secretly started to believe that Apricot and Mulberry had a point—babies really don't know *anything*! She had tried to leave Amy alone to look after Robbie herself, but Amy was asking for her help quite a lot these days. It was annoying Mulberry, who was barely speaking to Sam at the moment.

'It's not that I can't do any of this stuff with him,' explained Amy, pink in the face with embarrassment. 'It's just that I don't know how he is going to react to anything. I feel really nervous when I am on my own with him and I don't want him to sense it. Dawn said I had to be calm and confident at all times as he will look to me to be his leader. It's just easier said than done. I feel better when someone is with me.'

When Amy said she didn't know how Robbie was going to react to anything, she wasn't joking. Just leading him through the yard was an event in itself. Sam couldn't talk to him properly in front of Amy because no one else knew she could talk to animals so she would just look strange. She had to let him get on with it. And Robbie really did react to everything!

Big things didn't seem to bother him. A car drove through the yard one day as liveries left to go home and Sam tensed up, waiting for Robbie to panic. But he barely glanced at the machine as it slid past him, its engine rumbling. But then a crisp packet dropped by a careless child tumbled across his path, twisting over and over, and he jumped back as if he'd had another electric shock, eyes

bulging from their sockets, nostrils flared, and panting with panic. Amy had to jump out of his way before he stood on her foot, and over the next three days, Robbie managed to thump down on Amy's toes several times.

Amy had decided not to ride Robbie straight away but to let him settle in a little first. It was a good idea. In no particular order, Robbie was frightened of: any kind of flapping rubbish, *especially* plastic bags; panting dogs (dogs that didn't pant were OK); very large flowerpots; bicycles; rabbits; cows; new objects in a place he'd passed the day before; and an ice-cream sign that kept squeaking as it swung gently on its hinges. The first time he came across that, Sam thought he was going to faint. He planted his big feet, shook like a leaf, flared his nostrils, widened his eyes, and refused to walk past it. Sam and Amy had to push and pull to get him to move, and it was only when he was level with the sign that he decided to move forward, cantering so suddenly that the sisters were dragged alongside him. Just trying to turn him to put him in the field normally left both girls trembling with nerves. He was as jittery as a kitten and as a big a rhino.

Although Sam had promised Mulberry she would have nothing to do with Robbie, he was taking up more and more of her time. She found that helping Amy meant she had less time to ride Mulberry. So often she was cutting their rides short, turning her for home and having to listen to Mulberry complain all the way back. She didn't take as long grooming her any more and she didn't have the time to hang about in her stable chatting if she wanted to get all her chores done before Mum came to pick them up. Mulberry was upset, she could tell. But for some reason, Mulberry didn't want to talk about Robbie. Sam was relieved as she didn't want to argue. So she carried on rushing about, trying to give

Mulberry as much attention as she could and kept her fingers crossed that Robbie and Amy would soon start doing things on their own.

She did try to hurry things along by sneaking up to Robbie's stable in the upper yard to try and talk through his fears. She hoped she could persuade him to be braver— but it wasn't as simple as that.

'What's your problem with cows, Robbie?' she asked. 'They're not much different from horses.'

'Ooh, they are,' said the baby pony, widening his eyes at her. 'They smell so bad and the way they stare at you and then all run down to the fence at once—' He broke off and shuddered. 'It's like they're all ganging up on me.'

Sam sighed. 'OK, well, why won't you walk past that bench by your field without leaping about?'

'What's a bench?' asked Robbie.

'You know, that grey, long thing that we pass.'

'Well, it just sits there!'

'And?'

'I don't know what it's up to.'

'It's a bench!' said Sam.

Robbie shook his forelock into his eyes and narrowed them at her. 'You keep saying that, like I should know what that means. But I DON'T, so you're not making me feel better.'

'Told you babies are trouble,' said a voice outside the door. Sam peered over and saw Apricot, Mickey, and Turbo looking up at her.

'What are you lot doing out?'

'Lunchtime, innit?' said Turbo. 'We thought we would sneak out of the barn and stretch our legs for a bit.'

'Let us in, then,' said Mickey.

Sam sighed and held the door open for the three of them to trot past her. They lined up in front of Robbie, who gazed down at them with a worried expression.

'Now listen, young 'un,' said Apricot in a stern tone of voice. 'You can't help being as brainless as a budgie. You need to get over your instincts as a prey animal. You get scared, you want to run away. But right now, you're scared of everything and it's a bit boring. You need to grow up quickly!'

Robbie glared at her. 'What's it got to do with you?'

'Ooh, bolshie!' said Mickey while Turbo giggled. 'Spoken like a proper native pony!'

'Because your amateur dramatics are disturbing my naps!' said Apricot. 'It was funny at first, but, like I said, you're getting boring. You haven't got the sense to open your eyes and look at what upsets you. Instead, you let those instincts take over and behave as though everything that's strange and new is a lion! We're domesticated now; we've two-legs to do our thinking for us!'

'What's a lion?' asked Robbie.

'It's a really, really massive cat that can jump on ponies!' said Turbo proudly.

'There are LIONS around here?!' asked Robbie, looking horrified.

'No, there are no lions!' said Sam. 'I think you lot had better go back to the barn— you're making things worse.' She held the door open and the Shetlands marched out, muttering under their breaths.

'How do you know so much about lions?'

she heard Mickey ask Turbo as they trotted away.

'One of the kids who grooms me at the weekends is always nattering on about this stuff,' said Turbo. 'She talks to me all day long without taking a breath. And I don't know whether half of it is true or not. Drives me mad, to be honest.'

'There are really no lions around here?' asked Robbie, looking at Sam suspiciously.

'No lions in the country at all,' said Sam, crossing her fingers behind her back against her lie. But she seriously doubted Amy would be taking Robbie to the zoo any time soon.

Sam knew that Amy wouldn't admit it to anyone, but she was finding how little Robbie knew frustrating. Take picking out his feet. Ponies and horses need to have their feet checked for stones and kept clean. With Velvet and Mulberry, all Sam and Amy had to do was run their hands down the front of their legs and say, 'Up!' and both mares would lift their hoofs, allowing them to be cleaned with a hoof pick. But Robbie had only just been taught this by Dawn and he didn't realize what Amy wanted the first day when he stood there looking blankly at her as she rubbed his legs and said, 'Up, up. UP!' Sam had watched from the doorway and tried not to giggle when all the blood rushed to Amy's face as she bent over, her hand on Robbie's hoof, waiting for him to lift his leg. When he finally realized what she wanted, he was so eager to please, he lifted his leg very fast and hit her in the face with his knee.

Robbie had the concentration span of a goldfish. He would forget that Amy was holding his leg while cleaning his feet and would try to take a step forward to sniff at something in his stable, losing his balance in the process and falling, hitting his sensitive nose on the wall. Amy thought it was very sweet, but it wasn't so adorable when he did the same thing later that week while being shod, and fell onto the farrier's apprentice.

As well as this they could add clumsy to the list. Robbie sat on things, chewed things, barged into things, and stood on things. But even though Sam was beginning to see him as a natural disaster, Amy was falling deeper and deeper in love. 'I know he's a pain,' she said, kissing him on the nose after having fished her mobile phone out of his mouth. 'But he's my pain.' She then fell over because Robbie, who had been playing with the zip on her riding boot, had decided to pull on it, hard.

Things came to head the day they tried to put a rug on him.

'Here, said Janey, their riding instructor, shoving a stable rug into Amy's hands. 'You need him to get used to having rugs taken on and off. If the weather gets really bad, he needs to be wearing them every day.'

'What do I do?' asked Amy.

'Fold the rug into quarters and hold it out in front of you,' said Janey. 'Talk to him in soothing tones and when you get near him, lay it on his back. He might walk around the stable a bit, but when he calms down, just start opening the rug up until it covers him. Then take it off him. You can try doing up the straps on him tomorrow.'

'Why is putting a rug on him going to be such a big deal?' asked Sam.

'Horses and ponies are prey animals,' said Janey. 'Predators normally jump onto their backs to wrestle them to the ground so anything moving above their heads or lying on their backs upsets them, and their first instinct is to run in case it's a predator. You should see how most youngsters react to getting a saddle strapped onto them for the first time.'

Robbie pressed himself against the back wall of his stable and snorted nervously as Amy walked in with the rug over her arm. She did just as Janey said, talking to him in soft and soothing tones and letting him sniff

the strange object in her arms to calm him. But as she was doing this, one of the biggest spiders Sam had seen in her life walked out from the folds of the rug and began to tiptoe up Amy's arm. Amy froze and Robbie's whole body went tense with fear.

'Stay calm!' hissed Janey from the doorway. 'If you get scared, he'll get scared. It's just a spider.'

'I'm scared of spiders!' whispered Amy in a terrified squeak as the insect crept closer and closer to her shoulder.

'Keep going, put the rug on him,' whispered Janey as Robbie started to tremble. 'Don't let him think the rug is what is scaring you.'

'I can't,' said Amy, tears filling her eyes as the spider began to inch past her elbow. 'Come in here and get it off me!'

'I can't,' said Janey.

'Why not?' asked Amy.

'I'm terrified of spiders too!' said Janey.

The spider decided to put on a burst of speed and scuttle up toward Amy's shoulder. Amy screamed, threw the rug on the ground, and began beating at her arm while yelling, 'Get it off, get it off, get it OFF!' Robbie panicked and began to run around the stable after Amy, snorting and kicking at the rug. Janey reached in and pulled Amy through the open door before slamming it on a hysterical Robbie.

'Well,' said Sam. 'That went well.'

It was another month before Robbie would let them put a rug on his back.

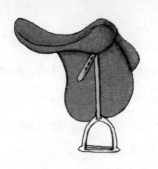

Chapter 7

The next day, Miss Mildew, the owner of Meadow Vale Riding School, had cornered Sam and Amy when they were cleaning Mulberry and Velvet's saddles and bridles in the tack room. Her long, pointy shadow loomed over them and both girls shuddered under her icy gaze.

'Miss Grey, I think you have given Robbie plenty of time to settle in,' said Miss Mildew to Amy. 'You're going to ride him today.'

'Oh, I can't,' said Amy. 'I don't have a saddle for him yet. Sorry.'

'You may borrow one from the riding school until you get your own.'

'I think he could do with a couple of days

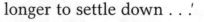

longer to settle down . . .'

'He is as settled as he is going to get,' said Miss Mildew. 'He needs to be doing something or he will get bored. A bored pony is a naughty pony. I will not tolerate a badly behaved animal on this yard; it reflects badly on the reputation of the riding school. You WILL ride him today, Miss Grey, and you will do a good job of it,' said Miss Mildew as she walked off.

Amy looked down at her hands and sighed. 'Let's get this over with.'

Sam looked at her in surprise. 'Don't you want do ride him?'

'After what happened yesterday with the rug, I'm scared of what he will do when he

78

feels my weight on his back,' admitted Amy. 'I hardly got any sleep last night thinking about it.'

Sam's jaw dropped open as she looked at her big sister in shock. Sam had always looked up to Amy—happy, confident Amy who found everything so easy when Sam always seemed to struggle. She never thought she would hear Amy say she was frightened to do something. She certainly never thought Amy would be scared of riding anything. There wasn't a horse or pony at Meadow Vale that Amy couldn't ride—including Mulberry!

Amy groaned. 'Oh, Sam, don't look at me like that! I'm not the perfect rider you think I am. I've got to be honest, it's a shock how little a youngster knows, how much they overreact to things that older horses walk past without a second glance. It makes me a bit nervous about getting on him.'

'Why don't I get Janey to come and help?' asked Sam. 'If we both stayed with you, would that make you feel better?'

'I don't think he's going to do anything I can't handle,' said Amy. 'But, yeah, it would be nice to have some company.'

Janey was happy to help when they asked her. 'You have to get on him or the fear will just build up in your mind until you can't move,' she said. 'Get up on him now and the two of you will be cantering through the fields before you know it!'

Sam was supposed to be riding Mulberry that morning and she did feel a little guilty at letting the mare down and then rushing her through the yard and out to the field. Mulberry grumbled a little about two-legs who didn't keep to their routines, but Sam consoled her with a kiss on the nose and the promise of an extra apple. Then she hurried back to the stables and rushed about helping

Janey and Amy get Robbie ready. Amy was as calm and steady as she always was, but as she finished buckling up the girth, Sam noticed she was frowning.

'Don't be nervous, Amy,' said Sam. 'I really think he wants to make you happy. I'm sure he is going to be a good boy.'

'Do you think so?' asked Amy as she stroked Robbie's soft nose and he gazed at her adoringly. 'You always seem to know what they are thinking, Sam. I wish ponies understood what we are saying and that we could talk to them like we do with people. Life would be a lot easier if I knew what was going on inside his head.'

Sam shrugged. 'We can only trust each other. Isn't that what Mum and Janey are always saying?'

Amy sighed and gathered Robbie's reins in her hands. 'You're right. I have to start somewhere with him.'

Sam trailed behind her sister down to the school, where Janey was waiting for them. Not for the first time she wondered why she was the only one who seemed to be able to hear animals talking and they understood her. She would give anything for Amy to have the same talent, even if it was only for the next half an hour.

Janey was waiting for them with a long lead rope in her hands. Robbie walked into the school. He was quiet and careful and stood looking around as they talked.

'Sam is going to hold the stirrup as you get on so the saddle doesn't move on his back,' said Janey. 'I'm going to clip this lead rope to his bit and the two of us are going to walk around with you, one on each side. That is all we are going to do today, walk around.'

Amy nodded and swung herself easily into the saddle. Sam smiled to see how steady Amy's hands were on the reins, how confidently she sat in the saddle, her long legs loose and relaxed against Robbie's sides.

Off they all went, walking loops and circles around the school, patting and reassuring Robbie as he took each step. 'How do you feel?' Janey asked Amy.

'Good,' said Amy. 'He seems lovely and calm and he is so comfortable to ride.'

'OK, let go, Sam,' said Janey. Sam stopped and let Robbie and Amy walk on without her. Janey stepped back and let the lead rope stretch out between herself and Robbie. 'I'll be right here and I'll tell him to stop with this rein if things get scary,' she said. On Amy went, looking more and more like her old self as Robbie walked around the arena. Her smile got bigger and bigger and she urged him into a trot. Robbie looked surprised and did an odd, skipping trot, then ducked his head down and started shaking it, his beautiful mane frothing like a wave.

'What's he doing?' asked Amy, a trace of nerves creeping back into her voice.

Janey laughed. 'He's excited! Perhaps build up slowly to trotting in the school, eh?'

Amy grinned and slowed Robbie down to a walk before halting him in the middle of the school. Sam and Janey gathered round and all three of them patted him and praised him, while Robbie wriggled with delight at all the attention.

'What a lovely boy you have, Amy,' said Janey. 'Calm, sensible, eager to please. He's going to be a fantastic youngster to work with.' Just as she said that, Robbie gave a huge yawn.

'How can he be tired after only fifteen minutes?' asked Amy.

'Little and often with babies, Amy. It will be a couple of years before he can work like Velvet,' said Janey. 'Why don't you take him back to his stable? Tomorrow I think you should try a short ride, say half an hour, with Sam and Mulberry.'

'Mulberry?' she asked. 'Why do you want him to go out with Mulberry?'

'He needs a babysitter when he first starts to hack,' said Janey. 'An older, confident pony he can take the lead from. A baby isn't confident enough to go anywhere on their own at first—they prefer having someone to follow. Mulberry is as steady as a rock out on a ride—she will make a perfect lead pony.'

'I'm not sure about that,' said Sam as she pictured how furious Mulberry was going to be when she found out she was expected to be Robbie's babysitter. 'I think Velvet would be better—why don't you go out with Mum and Velvet instead?'

'Oh, come on, Sam, it will be so much fun,' pleaded Amy. 'It's what we always dreamed of doing, going out for rides on our own.'

Sam looked up into her sister's happy face

and felt trapped. How on earth could she say no to Amy? She was just going to have to put up with the almighty temper tantrum Mulberry was bound to throw.

'Sure,' she said. 'Let's go tomorrow morning. It will be fun.'

'That's what I like to see,' said Janey as she walked out of the school. 'Both my students happy and smiling.'

Sam helped Amy put Robbie back in his stable and tidied up all the grooming kit and tack. She watched as Amy threw her arms around Robbie's neck and kissed him on the nose.

'Do you feel better, then?' she asked.

'Honestly, I don't know what I was worried about in the first place,' said Amy. 'He is such a sweet pony. It was so silly of me.'

'Not really,' said Sam, leaning on the stable door and propping her chin up on her arms.

'He's very different from what we are used to. It made you wobble for a bit, that's all. But you're happy now?'

Amy hugged Robbie again, her face lit up with a huge smile. 'Very happy. Let me put my hat and boots away and I'll phone home and tell them we are ready to be picked up.'

Sam stepped aside to let Amy out of the stable and then settled her chin on her arms again as she gazed at Robbie.

'You were such a good boy today,' she said.

He yawned, his dark eyes half shut and blinking. 'That was exhausting,' he said. 'I need a nap.'

Sam giggled as he knelt down and then flopped onto his side in his bed of clean, sweet-smelling wood shavings.

'Have a big sleep,' she said. 'Tomorrow is going to be a really big day. We are going to leave the yard.'

Robbie struggled to keep his eyes open. 'We're going Outside? That will be fun . . .' He interrupted himself with a jaw-popping yawn. 'Maybe we could go fast, have a bit of a . . .' he yawned again, '. . . canter.' Sam

watched his creamy chin drop onto his chest and his eyelids close as he gave a contented sigh. She waited until the stable began to vibrate with his snores and then she tiptoed away.

Chapter 8

Sam wasn't looking forward to telling Mulberry she was going to be babysitting Robbie that day. It was a pity to spoil her good mood and Mulberry was looking quite calm and cheerful as she waited for Sam to bring her breakfast that morning. Suspiciously so.

'Isn't it lovely today?' she asked Sam. 'The sun is shining, the birds are singing, and it's the perfect day to go for a ride.'

Sam narrowed her eyes. 'You've heard all about it, haven't you? Who told you?'

'What, that I have to babysit?' said Mulberry. 'Of course I've heard! The whole bloomin' yard is having a laugh at my expense. Plus, I had Gob Almighty giving me a lecture in the field last night about behaving myself.'

'Who, Velvet?' asked Sam as Mulberry tucked into her morning hay net. 'Well, she's right, he's just a baby, and, like Velvet said, you were all like that once.'

Mulberry snorted. 'I was nothing like

him. The farmer opposite let some cows out into his fields the day before yesterday and, I swear, Robbie looked ready to pass out on the spot! I mean, what has he got against cows? They're vegetarian, just like us. He'd be better off worrying about those two weasels, Mike and Mindy. They can be really dangerous.'

'Why, what have they done?' asked Sam.

'I don't know, but it's bound to be something,' said Mulberry.

Sam rolled her eyes. 'That makes no sense.'

'They're predators and you just can't trust a predator,' said Mulberry. 'If they get hungry, there is a whole yard full of prey animals for them to snack on.'

'How are they going to do that?' asked Sam. 'They're tiny; they couldn't bring down a Shetland.'

Mulberry leaned her head over her stable door, looked from side to side to see if anyone was listening, and lowered her voice to a whisper. 'I reckon they climb up onto our necks while we are sleeping and suck our blood out. That's been their plan all along; it's why they were so keen to come to the yard. I have a few bite marks on *my* neck already.'

'You probably have fleas again,' said Sam.

'That's what they *want* you to think,' said Mulberry.

Not for the first time since meeting Mulberry, Sam could only marvel at the way that she could wander off onto a completely different subject. There were times when Sam wondered if Mulberry was even on the same planet.

'Do you remember what we are supposed to be doing today?' asked Sam.

'Of course I do,' said Mulberry. 'We're babysitting the Witless Wonder.'

'Mulberry, be nice!' said Sam. 'I mean it.

Robbie needs your help and this means a lot to Amy. She loves Robbie and we love her.'

'We do?' asked Mulberry.

'Yes, we do,' said Sam. 'So you *are* going to be good.'

'Fine, fine, fine,' grumbled Mulberry. 'What do I get out of it?'

'My everlasting love?' said Sam.

'I get that anyway,' said Mulberry. 'If you want me to be nice, you had better sweeten the deal.'

'How about an apple?'

'I always get one of those after a ride. What else have you got?'

'Two apples.'

'Tempting, but not tempting enough.'

'How about some hard feed?'

'Pony nuts?'

'You're on.'

'Make it two scoops and you have a deal.'

'No way! I'll do half a scoop.'

'Make it a whole one and we can stop this tedious conversation.'

'Deal!' Sam leaned over the stable door and scratched Mulberry under the chin. The little mare closed her eyes and sighed with contentment. 'You know we can't have a lot of fun on this ride, don't you, Mulberry? No cantering or galloping and we can't be out for too long.'

'You never can with babies—they have no stamina,' said Mulberry. 'It's why no one ever wants to babysit.'

'Well, how about we go on a hack all by ourselves tomorrow? We can have loads of fun, just you and me. It will give you a chance to work off that scoop of pony nuts.'

'Sounds good,' said Mulberry. 'We're not going to have to go out with the Witless Wonder all the time, are we?'

'No, and stop calling him that. His name is Robbie,' said Sam, while Mulberry snorted with disdain. 'Now hurry up and eat your breakfast. You're on babysitting duty in an hour.'

As Sam walked away to get her tack, she heard Mulberry sigh. 'I suppose I should be grateful I'm getting to spend time with you.' Sam felt guilty, but she kept walking, not wanting to fight with Mulberry.

As soon as Robbie settles, I'll make it up to Mulberry, Sam thought.

Chapter 9

They had decided to use a little track that connected the fields around the yard. This also meant they didn't have to ride in traffic—which was fine by Amy and Robbie.

But it wasn't as easy to go for the ride as they had thought. As soon as they left the familiar surroundings of the yard, Robbie planted his feet and refused to move. Amy squeezed with her legs and gave him a firm kick when that didn't work, and even a little tap with her riding whip, but he ignored everything. He just looked all around him with his eyes wide and it was as if she wasn't even on his back.

'What's wrong with him?' asked Sam.

'I don't know,' said Amy. 'He's not listening to me at all.'

'He's probably just a bit scared,' said Sam. 'I'll trot on with Mulberry. He'll probably follow us.' She clicked her tongue and Mulberry trotted off. After about a minute, she heard Amy calling her and she looked over her shoulder. Robbie hadn't moved!

Mulberry sighed as Sam turned her head to bring them back. 'You should have brought a packed lunch.'

'Didn't I tell you to be nice?'

'I don't see how pointing out the obvious makes me horrible,' said Mulberry.

'Talk to him, would you?' asked Sam as they walked up to Robbie. Mulberry cocked her head and glared at him.

'What's wrong with you?'

'It's just that it's all so big,' said the baby Highland, his eyes as round as saucers in his

face. 'Everything smells so different—and all the noise!'

'Yes, well, that's because we are Outside,' said Mulberry. 'Get used to it.'

Robbie stared at her. 'How am I supposed to do that?'

'Isn't it cute, the way they sound as though they are talking to each other?' said Amy. Sam smiled weakly.

'Look, I suggest you start putting one hoof in front of the other, otherwise you are going to find yourself back at that stud faster than you can blink,' said Mulberry. 'Just follow my tail and do what I do. If I don't spook at something, it's not scary. But if you see me running past you, yelling my head off, that would be a good moment to work yourself up into a gallop. OK?'

Robbie looked at Mulberry suspiciously. 'You're not going to try and trick me?'

'It's tempting, but I'd like to get back to

my stable and my dinner before I die of old age!' snapped Mulberry.

Robbie snorted and when Sam turned Mulberry around and asked her to trot on, he followed. 'Thank goodness,' said Amy. 'I thought I was going to be there all day!'

Sam leaned down and patted Mulberry on the neck. 'Good girl!'

'I haven't the patience for this,' grumbled Mulberry.

They hadn't ridden more than a few yards when Robbie stopped dead again and stared at a bench that had been placed by the track so walkers could sit and enjoy the view across the hills. Amy tried to nudge him past with her legs but he just whispered, 'What is it?'

'It's OK, Robbie, it's just a bench,' said Amy, patting his neck.

Robbie looked at Mulberry in panic. 'They all keep saying that, but what IS IT?'

Mulberry sighed. 'It's just a thing two-legs

sit on, because they're lazy like that.'

'Is it dangerous?' asked Robbie.

'Weeeell,' said Mulberry. 'They have been known to pull themselves up from their supports and run after ponies.'

Robbie stared at Mulberry, terrified. 'What happens if they catch you?'

'No one has ever come back to tell us,' said Mulberry.

Robbie gave a snort and bounded past the bench, tucking his tail between his legs as he tried to get away from it as fast as possible.

'Now that was naughty, Mulberry,' scolded Sam as they jogged along to catch up.

Mulberry snorted. 'It got him moving, didn't it? Besides, I'm beginning to enjoy myself now.'

Robbie's walk and trot was painfully slow as his head constantly moved from side to side and his nostrils flared wide, taking in every scent around him. Every rustle in the bushes made him jump, and when they came to some evergreen trees that threw the track into a deep shadow, he had to be coaxed under their leaves.

But the next obstacle that terrified him turned out to be a young pheasant. Sam found pheasants to be really stupid birds. They never flew if they could help it, even though they had wings. They tended to get under Mulberry's hoofs because they always froze when something frightened them, rather than getting out of the way. This pheasant had stopped right in the middle of the track and was staring at them. Mulberry walked past it, but when Sam turned to check on Amy and Robbie, the baby Highland had frozen again.

'I don't believe this,' sighed Amy.

'At least your nerves are gone,' said Sam as Robbie spread his front legs and bent his head low to the ground to sniff at the

pheasant, his whole body tense and ready to spring away if it went for him.

'Come on, Robbie,' said Amy, giving him a sharp kick to make him move. The muscly little tank of a pony gave no sign he had felt it. He continued to goggle and snort at the pheasant, who had also decided he wasn't moving. Robbie stood up again and tentatively stretched one hoof out to take a step and then snatched his leg back again when the pheasant moved his head. Cautiously, the pheasant took a step away and then another, moving slowly and carefully, still on the track, still right in the middle of it. No matter how much Amy urged him forward, Robbie was too scared to walk past the pheasant and catch up with Mulberry. Slowly, slowly, slowly the pheasant and Robbie inched their way up the track, eyeing each other in terror.

Mulberry looked on in disgust. 'If he walks any slower, he's going to fall over,' she said.

'Well, say something to him then,' whispered Sam.

'This is ridiculous,' said Mulberry. 'I can't stand small talk—I'm not the chatty type.'

'You could have fooled me,' said Sam under her breath.

'What was that?' asked Mulberry.

'Nothing,' said Sam.

'What is wrong with you now?' asked Mulberry as she stomped up to Robbie. Caught between two ponies, the poor pheasant flattened himself against the ground and screwed his eyes up tight.

'It looks weird,' said Robbie. 'And it smells weird. I don't want to go past it and turn my back on it.'

'Probably wise,' said Mulberry.

Sam coughed loudly and tried to drown Mulberry out, but she hadn't distracted Robbie. 'Why? Why is it wise not to turn my back on it?'

'That's a pheasant, that is,' said Mulberry. The bird opened one eye and peeked up at Mulberry. 'They look harmless enough, but they have these fangs hidden in their beaks. They're too small to tackle a pony head-on, but turn your back on them and they leap up and sink those fangs into you.'

'Then what?' asked Robbie.

'They suck all your blood out until all that's left is a husk of dried-up old leather with a scrap of mane and tail attached to it,' said Mulberry.

'Stop it!' hissed Sam.

'Stop what?' asked Amy.

'Why aren't you scared of it?' asked Robbie, looking terrified.

'Oh, I'm too old for a pheasant,' said Mulberry. 'They only like young ponies.'

At that, poor Robbie gave a snort of fear, spun on his back hoofs, and set off for home at a smart trot. 'I think it's time we went back—he's had enough,' called Amy over her shoulder. The pheasant finally flew away with a whirr of its wings, disturbing the silence beneath the trees with his grating call.

'That was a really horrible thing to do,' said Sam.

'I'm just teasing him,' said Mulberry as she trotted after them. 'Besides, it made the ride much more fun.'

'Only for you,' said Sam.

'If he's going to live on a big yard, he needs to take a bit of teasing and see the funny side of things,' said Mulberry.

'It's only funny if everyone is laughing, Mulberry. That means Robbie too,' said Sam.

Mulberry thought about this for a second. 'Nope, I have to disagree with you on that one; this is still pretty funny. Are we doing this again tomorrow?'

Not if I can get out of it, thought Sam.

Chapter 10

Once Amy realized that Robbie wasn't going to bolt in a blind panic, buck, or rear when something upset him, she was much more eager to ride him. 'Let's go through the village today and take Mulberry and Robbie onto the bridle path; we'll see if we can get Robbie to canter,' she said to Sam over breakfast. Sam almost choked on her cornflakes.

'Um, I fancied just staying in the school with Mulberry today,' said Sam, crossing her fingers under the table. 'Why don't you go out with Mum and Velvet?'

'I can't today,' said Mum as she buttered a slice of toast. 'I have to pick up Robbie's new saddle so I'll be gone most of the morning.'

'Why don't you take Robbie into the arena instead?' asked Sam, but Amy just pulled a face.

'I think he needs to be fitter before I start schooling him,' she said.

'Amy's right,' said Mum. 'Robbie is unfit and his bones are still growing and developing.

The school is hard work on a pony. All that bending and flexing through corners, it's like going to the gym for us. Much better for him to build up his fitness on hacks.'

'Sure,' Sam said after she had thought about it. 'A hack will be fun.' Mulberry would probably disagree, but if she was going to have to get used to riding with Robbie and Amy, the sooner the better, Sam decided.

Mulberry, though, was suspiciously happy when Sam went to give her a breakfast hay net.

'Are we on babysitting duty again today?' she asked.

Sam looked at her out of the corner of her eye. 'Yes, we are. Don't be angry about it.'

'Angry? I'm looking forward to it!' said Mulberry.

Sam frowned at her. 'What's made you change your mind about Robbie?'

'Nothing. I still think he's as thick as a

cowpat,' said Mulberry. 'But everyone is loving the stories about his ride-outs. I told the whole field that story about the pheasant six times last night and it got a laugh every time!'

'Did Robbie hear this?' asked Sam.

'I think he heard it the first couple of times. Didn't seem to mind, though,' said Mulberry.

'I bet he did,' said Sam.

Mulberry sighed. 'I keep telling you, every pony that comes onto a new yard has to put up with a bit of teasing. I got teased when I first came up here and I was fine about it,' said Mulberry.

Sam rolled her eyes, but she kept her thoughts to herself.

'By Christmas, he'll be settled in,' said Mulberry. 'But it would help if Velvet stopped mollycoddling him all the time. He won't grow a thick skin if she keeps treating him like a foal. I think you should have a word.'

'I won't!' said Sam. 'From the sound of things, he needs someone in the field who doesn't tease him.'

Now it was Mulberry's turn to roll her eyes.

'I mean it,' said Sam. 'Don't tease him too much. You and the Shetlands, you go too far sometimes.'

'Do not compare me to that horrible little bunch,' said Mulberry. 'Apricot is proper spiteful. She should have been kicked off the yard years ago.'

'You're all heart, Mulberry, did you know that?' asked Sam, not bothering to keep the sarcasm from her voice.

'I'm a diamond in the rough, me,' said Mulberry. 'People just don't appreciate me. Where are we going today, anyway?'

'Amy wants to take Robbie out onto the bridle path and see if we can have a canter through the fields,' said Sam. 'That means riding on the road through the village to get to the bridle path so you need to give him lots of confidence today.'

'The road, eh?' Mulberry's eyes gleamed with delight. 'That will be fun.'

Sam looked at her suspiciously. 'Why should it be fun? You're not planning on doing anything to him, are you?'

'Me? Wouldn't dream of it.'

'I mean it, Mulberry—be good!'

'I won't put a hoof wrong,' said Mulberry.

'Promise?'

'Promise.'

'Cross your heart and hope to die?' asked Sam. 'Stick a needle in your eye, if you tell a lie?'

'I still don't know what a needle is so it doesn't seem fair to make a promise that involves one but, yes, I *promise* I am going to be good,' said Mulberry.

Sam sighed and finished tidying up Mulberry's hay net before tacking her up. Amy had brought Robbie in from the field and was grooming and tacking him up on the upper yard while she chatted to her friends. Sam was feeling lazy, so she mounted up and let Mulberry carry her through the yard, her reins long and slack in her hands

as she tipped her head back to enjoy the bright winter sunshine. Robbie was ready and standing by the mounting block outside the office.

'Could you hold him for a sec?' Amy asked Sam. 'I forgot to put my hat on.'

'Sure.' Sam jumped down from Mulberry with what she hoped was the same easy grace as her big sister and held out her hand for Robbie's reins while Amy walked off to the tack room.

'I'm going to be good today,' said Robbie in a firm voice.

'You were a good boy yesterday,' Sam reassured him. 'You can't listen to everything Mulberry says; she does like to tease you. But she doesn't mean it, do you, Mulberry?'

'Oh, for heaven's sake,' said Mulberry. 'Look young 'un, it was a joke, all that stuff I told you about the pheasant and the bench. You're a newbie, so you're going to get a bit of teasing until everyone gets used to you.'

'That's easy for you to say,' said Robbie, looking up at her from beneath his shaggy forelock.

Mulberry shrugged. 'You'll soon settle in and be one of the herd, newbie,' she said, but Sam thought she could see a guilty look in her eyes.

'You made out like I did a really bad job of the ride yesterday,' said Robbie, getting huffier by the second.

'Oh, for goodness' sake!' said Mulberry. 'You didn't drop your rider, did you? Try not to drop her today and I'm sure there'll be a medal or something in it for you.'

'Really?' Robbie brightened up. 'Like a rosette?'

'Yes,' said Sam. 'You can have one of Mulberry's.' She stuck her tongue out at the little mare who had laid her ears back against her head in anger.

'Where are we going today?' asked Robbie. Sam thought he sounded a little worried. 'Are we going near any pheasants?'

'We're going on the road,' said Mulberry.

'What's a road?' asked Robbie.

Mulberry sniggered. 'This is going to be great!'

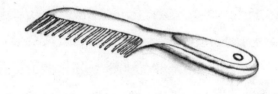

Chapter 11

Robbie was obviously not as stupid as Mulberry made him out to be because he didn't need reminding about tucking in behind Mulberry and following her lead down the road. Sam kept looking over her shoulder to talk to Amy and she could see his ears flicking backwards and forwards as he listened to them and his eyes looking all around him. He seemed to be concentrating much better today and was happy to be off the yard.

They did have one heart-stopping moment when a delivery truck came around the corner and parked outside a house with its engine running. This meant they had to ride around it to stay on their side of the road, and Sam worried that Robbie would get upset at something so big, rumbling away. But Amy put one hand on his neck and spoke to him in a soft voice, praising him with every step he took. Although he was very slow, the baby Highland walked past with no fuss, even if he did keep throwing anxious glances at the truck. Once they got past it, Amy patted him and praised him loudly. He bobbed his head as she talked to him, and Sam couldn't help but notice he had the funniest expression on his face. Every time Amy praised him his eyes softened and he had a happy, almost goofy look on his face. *He really wants to please Amy*, thought Sam. *He is a little sweetie.*

Meeting something as big as that truck and wondering how Robbie was going to react had been the one thing that had been worrying Sam all morning. She was always relieved when they got off the road even though her pony was very used to traffic. She thought Amy was very brave because, as sweet as Robbie was, Sam didn't think she would be confident riding him around cars. She would worry about what could happen far too much and poor Robbie would pick up on this and be a nervous wreck. Even though she wasn't riding him, as soon as they got away from that truck she felt her worry lifting from her shoulders, and she and Amy talked and laughed loudly in their relief. Both ponies picked up on their happier mood and walked on more smartly, lifting their knees just a little higher, a bounce in their step.

It was all going so well. Sam was looking forward to getting onto the bridle path and going for a canter and blowing the cobwebs away. But then they turned the corner and were confronted with a small army of bright orange traffic cones.

Sam stopped Mulberry and gaped at the scene before them. Workmen were digging up the road and not only were there about a hundred traffic cones clustered along the side of the road, but there were temporary road signs, a cement mixer churning round and round, and a man with a drill digging up chunks of tarmac. She looked over her shoulder at Robbie who had skittered out into the middle of the road as he tried to get away from the cones and was now frozen, staring at them wide-eyed and unblinking. Amy was red in the face with embarrassment and was desperately urging him forward, but, just like yesterday, he seemed to forget that she was even there. The village was normally very quiet, but there were already three cars waiting patiently behind Robbie, unable to get around him in the narrow country lane.

'You knew about this, didn't you?' Sam hissed at Mulberry.

The mare looked over her shoulder. 'One of the big horses *may* have mentioned something about roadworks when they came back in from a ride yesterday evening, yes.'

'You could have said something, Mulberry! He's frozen again.'

Mulberry looked at Robbie and sniggered. 'So he has. And he's causing the first traffic jam this place has ever seen.'

'Mulberry!'

'Oh, relax!' Mulberry huffed. 'It's only traffic cones. It's not like they could do anything to hurt him.'

'Yes, but he doesn't know that, does he?' said Sam.

Amy had dismounted and led Robbie to the side of the road. She put her hand up and mouthed a 'sorry' at each driver that went past, then led Robbie over to a traffic cone. He seemed happy to move along now that Amy was walking by his side.

'Look,' she said, grabbing the cone and plonking it down in front of his hoofs while the workmen looked on in amazement. 'It's just plastic—it's not going to do anything to you!'

Robbie carefully stretched out his nose and touched the very tip of the cone, before jumping back in case it bit him. When it didn't move, he stepped a tiny bit closer and sniffed at it again. His body started to relax as he sniffed it from its tip to its base and up again.

He was taking so long, Mulberry was getting bored again. 'Did you remember to bring a packed lunch today?' she asked Sam.

'Oh, stop it!' said Sam crossly.

After he had carefully sniffed every inch of the cone and Amy had patted him and talked to him, Robbie finally opened his mouth and began to chew on the cone, a sure sign he was comfortable with it. Amy gently took it out of his mouth and mounted up again.

'Do you want to keep going?' asked Sam.

'He's got to get used to stuff like this, so I'm glad it's all here. Let's ride them both past it.'

Sam nudged Mulberry forward with her knees and the little mare walked calmly past the roadworks. Robbie crept along behind, flinching at every sound, still keeping a wary eye on the cones. Just as they reached the end of the army of cones and Sam thought they could relax, a huge lorry loaded up with building supplies rumbled around the corner. He saw the ponies and pulled in as tight as he could to the side of the road, but they still had to squeeze past him. Sam hated having to ride past big trucks and this was the second time today! Her heart was in her mouth and she tried to keep calm by breathing deeply and slowly and listening for Robbie's hoof steps behind them. *If anything is going to freak him out*, she thought, *this is going to be it.*

'Just breathe, just breathe, just breathe,' she heard a voice saying behind her. 'No fangs, no fur, that means no danger, just keep walking, just keep walking . . .' She realized it was Robbie—he was doing the same thing as she was to try and stay calm.

Sam breathed a huge sigh of relief when they got past the lorry and it gently drove away. She looked round at Amy. '*That* was scary!'

Both Amy and Robbie looked tired. 'Let's turn around, Sam, and go home,' said Amy.

'Seriously?' asked Sam, amazed that her speed demon of a sister was giving up the chance to go for a canter in the sunshine.

'Seriously,' said Amy. 'From here to the yard is normally a ten-minute ride, but it's taken us half an hour. Robbie's tired and I think he's seen enough of the world today. Let's try again tomorrow.'

Sam looked at Robbie. His doe eyes were heavy-lidded and his creamy neck was grey with sweat.

Amy patted Robbie's neck, then turned his head and walked in front of Mulberry and Sam. 'He'll get better.'

But as they started to walk past the traffic cones, the lorry that had just passed them began to back towards them, beeping loudly as it attempted to turn into a driveway. Cars idled in the road as they waited for it to get out of the way, and just at that moment, a helicopter flew overhead. Robbie froze again.

'I don't believe this,' said Amy as she tried to make him go forward. Sam and Mulberry drew level with them so Sam could see that Robbie had his eyes squeezed shut with fear. 'Make it all go away, make it all go away, make it all go away . . .' the baby Highland kept muttering over and over again.

A tractor was driving slowly up the road behind them and the huge lorry was still reversing slowly. Cars were building up and Sam was starting to feel a bit scared.

'You're going to have to get off him and walk him through it all, Amy,' she said. 'I don't think he is going to go otherwise.'

'No way!' said Amy, her face white. 'What if he panics? I have more control if I stay in the saddle; otherwise he could pull the reins out of my hand and run off. If he is loose on the road, there could be a serious accident.'

'We can't stay here,' said Sam as Robbie continued to mutter away with his eyes shut. 'We're in the way!'

'I know that, I'm not blind!' snapped Amy.

'This is pure comedy gold,' said Mulberry happily. Sam rolled her eyes.

Just then, an impatient car driver decided to honk his horn, long and loud! Poor Robbie squealed with fright and leapt sideways, crashing through the traffic cones and landing in the freshly poured concrete. Sam gasped in horror as Robbie floundered about, splashing grey concrete all over himself, and the workmen shouted as poor Amy tugged desperately on the reins.

'Young 'un, listen to me,' called Mulberry in a clear, strong voice Sam hadn't heard her use before. 'It's nothing to worry about!'

'It's horrible,' squealed Robbie. 'It's all over me!'

'I'm not scared of it, am I?' said Mulberry.

'You're not in it!' said Robbie.

Mulberry walked over and plonked one hoof in the concrete, which made the workmen yell a bit more. Mulberry looked Robbie in the eye. 'Am I bothered?'

He stopped floundering and looked at her. 'No, no, you're not.'

'Remember what I said to you,' said Mulberry in a calm, low voice. 'If I'm not scared of it, nor should you be.'

'You're not trying to trick me?' he asked, his breathing still shallow and quick with fear.

Mulberry shook her head. 'I'm not trying to trick you. Just walk out of it. You'll be fine.'

'Don't worry, girls, I'll walk you through,' said one of the workmen, walking over to them. Sam watched open-mouthed as the man clapped his palms against his thighs and whistled as if Robbie was a dog.

'Come on then, boy!'

Still panting with fear, Robbie looked at him. The man started to walk backwards, slapping his thighs and whistling. 'Shall we follow him?' Robbie asked Mulberry.

'Go ahead,' said Mulberry. 'As long as we get home without any major injuries, I'm happy.'

So that was how they got home, with the workman coaxing Robbie along as if he was a seventy-stone puppy, Robbie walking after him nervously, and Amy sitting in the saddle, tomato-red with embarrassment as the surrounding motorists laughed. Mulberry gave Robbie the odd nudge from time to time when he looked as through he was going to hesitate or even stop. Amy said, 'Thank you!' politely to the man when they got past the lorry and then urged Robbie into a trot until they got to the driveway of the yard, where she asked him to stop. She turned to Sam.

'We are never going to talk about this again, OK?'

Sam nodded.

'And we're not hacking out again until those roadworks are gone, OK?'

Again, Sam nodded.

Amy breathed a sigh of relief. 'Good. Let's hope no one from the yard saw that. Thank goodness for Mulberry—she was so calm.' Amy put both reins in one hand and leaned over to scratch the little mare behind the ears. 'You are such a good girl, aren't you?' Sam smiled as Mulberry wriggled with pleasure.

Amy looked at her. 'Can you give me a hand getting this concrete off his legs before it sets?'

'Of course I can,' Sam replied.

Mulberry sighed. 'I'll just stand in the stable on my own again, shall I?' she grumbled.

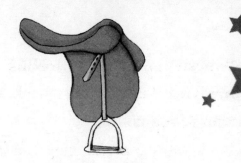

Chapter 12

Mulberry held her breath as they walked down to her stable on the bottom yard, and as soon as Sam let her through the door, Mulberry brayed with laughter like a donkey.

'That was hilarious!' she wheezed, as soon as she able to speak.

'It was not,' said Sam. 'Poor Robbie, he was so scared. You're not allowed to tell anyone about this, Mulberry.'

'Oh, come on,' said Mulberry. 'That's not fair.'

'No, what's not fair is letting the whole yard make fun of Robbie,' said Sam. 'He's really trying.'

Mulberry snorted in disgust.

'I mean it, Mulberry, BE NICE!'

Mulberry laid her ears back against her head. 'You're no fun!'

'Look, you were brilliant today, so I'll bring you some extra hay before I turn you out in the field.'

'Fine,' sulked Mulberry. 'But I want at least two armfuls.'

'OK, but you'll just have to wait a minute while I help Amy wash off Robbie's legs,' said Sam as she began to walk back towards Robbie's stable.

'You never said anything about waiting!' Mulberry called after her. 'Which I seem to do a lot these days!'

That made Sam feel a bit guilty so she decided to get Mulberry's hay first. As she walked up to the hay barns, she saw her mother's car pull into the car park. She ran over to get a kiss and a hug.

'Ooh, do you have Robbie's new saddle?' she asked.

'I certainly do,' said Mum. She opened the boot of the car and Sam rushed to look.

It was a soft, supple saddle made from dark brown leather and suede. The smell of new leather filled the car. Mum lifted it out and Sam noticed it flopped in an odd way over Mum's arm.

'Is it broken?' she asked.

Mum laughed. 'No Sam, it's a special saddle that has no rigid parts to it like an ordinary saddle. Robbie has another few years left before he is mature, and, because it's so soft, this saddle won't pinch or dig into him as he changes shape.'

Just then Amy walked around the corner, wet and tired-looking. She brightened up when she saw what Mum was holding.

'My new saddle!' she said. 'Let's try it!'

'I thought you said he was really tired?' said Sam.

'Oh, five minutes in the school won't hurt him,' said Amy.

'Well, tack him up quickly before he falls asleep,' said Mum.

Robbie looked surprised when Amy rushed into the stable with his new saddle.

He blinked at her with tired eyes and his expression seemed to say, *Really? I have to do this again?* Amy was already picking up on his moods and she patted him gently. 'Five minutes, Robbie, just to see if it fits. Then you can have a big sleep.'

She led him down to the school and mounted up. 'Just a little walk and trot, just to see that it fits and he is comfortable,' said Mum.

'Oh, this saddle is lovely,' said Amy as Robbie broke into a reluctant trot.

'What's it like?' said Sam.

'It's hard to describe,' said Amy. 'It's like riding bareback but much more comfortable.'

'So you like it?' asked Mum.

'It's great!' said Amy.

'Good,' said Mum. 'Robbie seems happy with it as well.'

'Come and try it, Sam,' said Amy.

Sam felt her heart sink. Amy was being

so generous, offering to let her sit on Robbie and try out her new saddle. It was an honour amongst riders. But she had promised Mulberry that she wouldn't ride Robbie. She had also promised Mulberry that she wouldn't spend any time with Robbie and she had already broken that promise. She didn't want to break another promise and hurt Mulberry's feelings—but she didn't want to hurt Amy's either!

Amy dismounted and held out the reins. 'Come on, Sam, what are you waiting for?'

Sam swallowed and looked around the yard as Mum and Amy stared at her.

'What's the matter, Sam?' asked Mum. 'You're not worried about getting up on Robbie because he's young, are you?'

Sam laughed nervously. 'Of course not.'

'Well, up you get then, you silly goose,' said Mum.

Sam walked down to the gate of the school,

double checking there was no one around who would see her get on Robbie. He was a bit big for her, so Amy gave her a leg up.

The saddle *was* lovely! The suede was so soft and warm and she could feel Robbie's back through it. It *was* like riding bareback, but without a knobbly spine sticking into her bum and with the comfort of knee rolls

and a big pommel to hold her in place, not to mention the stirrups. She asked Robbie to do another little trot around the school and she could feel his muscles rippling under the saddle. She could see why Amy was so confident on him already. He felt so different from Mulberry. She fizzed with energy, even when she was just walking and Sam always felt that any minute Mulberry would jump into a gallop. It used to scare her when she first started riding her. But Robbie loped along gently and, compared with Mulberry, he felt so calm and serene. She asked him to stop and reached down to pat his neck.

'You are a lovely, lovely pony,' she whispered in his ear. He bobbed his head and snorted with happiness.

A clatter of tiny hoofs made her look up and her heart sank as she saw Apricot, Mickey, and Turbo being led in from the field. They stopped at the gate and stared in at her, and

Sam was convinced she saw Apricot's eyes light up with malice.

'Um, I think he's had enough, Amy. Perhaps he should go for his nap now?' said Sam.

'Sure, I'll take him up,' said Amy. 'Do you want to give me a hand with him?'

'No, I was supposed to be giving Mulberry some hay and I need to finish grooming her,' said Sam.

'Hurry up then, and I'll give you both a lift home,' said Mum as Sam walked quickly out of the school.

Sam jogged off to get Mulberry's hay—she needed to finish up her jobs quickly so she could go home for dinner, but she wanted to spend a few minutes grooming Mulberry and telling her about riding Robbie. She knew Apricot would tell her if she didn't and she didn't want the Shetland winding Mulberry up by making a big deal of it.

But she was too late. As she walked over to Mulberry's stable with an armload of hay she could see the mare was in a bad mood. Apricot must have whispered the news of Sam's ride on Robbie to a pony as she passed its stable and, like Chinese whispers, the pony had passed the news onto its neighbour and they had passed it onto theirs, all the way through the yard until Mulberry's neighbour had whispered it into her ear.

'You promised!' said an indignant Mulberry, her tail swishing to and fro again like a cat's, while Sam dumped the hay in a corner of her stable. 'You promised you would NEVER ride him, but you did!'

'Don't be silly, Mulberry, I sat up on him for five minutes because Amy asked me to, that's all,' said Sam.

'I am NOT being silly,' said Mulberry, stamping her hoof. 'You've hardly had any time for me since he turned up and now you're *riding* him!'

'I'm helping out my sister while her new pony settles,' said Sam. 'You're overreacting!'

'You always say that!' said Mulberry. 'I only overreact because YOU don't LISTEN!' And with that, she turned her back on Sam, ignored the hay and faced the back wall, her angry tail swishing up a breeze.

'Fine,' said Sam. 'I'll talk to you tomorrow and I PROMISE, starting tomorrow, I'm spending all my time up here with you again. OK?'

Mulberry said nothing. Sam shook her head and sighed in frustration as she let herself out of the stable.

Chapter 13

The next morning brought more bad news. After a night spent in their stables, Janey had turned all the horses and ponies out into the field so they could kick up their heels and have a roll and a graze. Mum had been busy that morning and had not been able to give Sam and Amy a lift to the yard until lunchtime. But when they walked down to the field to fetch Robbie and Mulberry in and to get them ready for a ride, they found the electric fence was sagging in one place, its supports pulled free from the ground. While Velvet, Mulberry, and the Shetlands were happily grazing, Robbie was nowhere to be seen.

'Where is he?' asked Amy, scanning the nearby fields. But there was no sign of the little cream-coloured Highland.

Sam looked at the damaged fencing. 'You don't think . . . ?' she started to ask Amy as a horrible thought made her heart sink.

'I don't think what?' asked Amy.

Sam swallowed. 'You don't think he got through the fencing and then through the hedgerow in the next field, do you?'

Both girls looked at each other for a moment and then ran over the broken fencing into the next field and, sure enough, there was a large, Highland-shaped gap in the hedgerow. Tufts of creamy hair were caught on broken branches and the ground was littered with twigs and leaves. They gaped at it in shock.

'I don't believe it,' said Amy. 'That hedgerow is at least three feet thick. He must have charged at it to force his way through.'

Sam could only nod.

'He could be anywhere,' said Amy. 'He could be on the road, he could be hit by a car, anything!'

'He could be eating someone's garden,' said Sam hopefully.

Amy started to run back to the gate. 'We have to start looking for him!'

Sam let her sister run on ahead and walked

back into the first field, stepping carefully over the ribbons of electric fencing that still hummed with a charge.

'What happened?' she asked Velvet.

The big cob mare glared at the Shetlands, who all coughed and looked at the ground. 'I *told* you,' Velvet scolded. 'I told you it was a bad idea to teach him how to field-hop. Now look what's happened—he's run away!'

'No one actually told him to run through a hedgerow, though,' piped up Turbo in a scared voice. 'That was his idea.'

'It was you three, especially YOU, Turbo, that put the idea of escaping from the field into his head in the first place,' thundered Velvet as she stamped a hoof the size of a dinner plate. 'A baby that big will easily force himself through a hedgerow!'

'Why did he run away?' asked Sam, glancing at Mulberry who was still grazing and refusing to look in her direction, although Sam noticed her ears were flicking backwards and forwards as she followed the conversation.

'I don't know,' said Velvet. 'He was upset about the ride yesterday. Wouldn't tell anyone why, though, just wanted to graze on his own.'

'No one was teasing him?' asked Sam as Mulberry's ears flicked towards her.

'We thought about it,' said Apricot. 'But he was too miserable.'

Sam walked over to Mulberry and started buckling her head collar on.

'What are you going to do?' asked Velvet.

'I don't know,' said Sam as she started to lead Mulberry from the field. 'But we'll think of something.'

'In fairness, he could flatten a small car if he sat on the bonnet,' Apricot called after them. 'I reckon he'll be fine.'

It was action stations at the yard when Sam

walked onto it. Amy was crying in Janey's arms, Miss Mildew was on her mobile calling neighbours to see if Robbie had been spotted, while some very determined-looking riders were mounting up to go and look for him. Sam dragged Mulberry over to Amy so she could get a good look at how upset Amy was.

'Is Mum coming?' she asked Janey.

'She's on her way,' said Janey as she stroked Amy's hair. 'Don't you worry, we'll get him back.'

'Let's hope we get him back quickly,' said Miss Mildew. 'There is a big storm forecast for this evening and all the animals were going to be kept indoors tonight. It's not safe for that young pony to be out on his own and I dread to think what will happen if he is not back in his stable in the next two hours.'

Sure enough, the wind was beginning to get stronger, moaning as it dragged itself round the corners of stables and whipping up the dust and dirt on the dry ground. Amy began to cry harder while Janey went white with fear.

Sam swallowed. She practically ran with Mulberry down to her stable and rushed to get her tack.

'We're going to go and get him, aren't we?' Mulberry asked Sam, whose face was tight with worry.

'We can't leave him out in a storm, Mulberry,' said Sam. 'He could run out into a road, fall into a ditch and break his leg, or a tree could fall on him—anything could happen.'

Mulberry shuddered. 'I hate the wind. It goes right up my tail. We'll get the poor little fella back and then your mum can send him back to the stud.'

Sam looked at her, open-mouthed. 'Why?' she asked. 'Why on earth would we send him back?'

'Because,' said Mulberry, putting her nose in the air.

'Because WHAT, Mulberry?' asked Sam. 'Start talking—I'm not in the mood!'

'Because you'll end up loving him and forgetting me, that's why!' Mulberry said grumpily, her face a picture of misery. 'I'll be on my own and you'll spend all your time with HIM! You've already sat on his back.'

'For five minutes!' said Sam.

'That's how it starts!' said Mulberry. 'The odd ride here and there and then you start to think how much nicer to ride he is and how much better he is and then I get left in the stable ALL THE TIME!'

'No, you won't,' said Sam. 'Mulberry, we're bonded together. No one could ever replace you. But I'm part of a family, which means *you're* part of a family.'

'So?' asked Mulberry.

'So it's not just about you and me,' said

Sam. 'It's about Mum, Dad, Amy, Velvet, and now Robbie.'

'You can't love lots and lots of others,' said Mulberry. 'You can't say you love me and your parents and your sister *and* that bossy mare with all your heart and then someone new turns up and you say you love them as well. Your heart can't be full one day and then have room for another the next.'

Sam searched her pockets and pulled out a spare hair band. 'Look,' she said, stretching it slightly between two fingers. 'This is how much I love Amy, Mum, Dad, and Velvet.' Mulberry squinted down her long nose at Sam's hand. 'Then you came along.' Sam stretched the hair-band almost as wide as it could go. 'And my heart grew this big. Then Robbie came along.' She stretched it just a tiny, tiny bit more. 'And my heart grew a little more.'

Mulberry sighed and dropped her nose onto Sam's shoulder. 'I'm the biggest part of that hair band, though, right?'

'Yes, you are,' said Sam as she stroked Mulberry's face.

'I'm still number one?'

'Always,' said Sam.

Mulberry sighed again. 'Let's go and get this baby back before something bloomin' awful happens to him.'

'You sound like you have a plan,' said Sam.

'Of course,' said Mulberry. 'I'm not just drop-dead gorgeous, you know. I have brains too.'

'So, if you were Robbie, where would you go?' asked Sam.

'That's easy, I'd try and run back to the stud,' said Mulberry. 'But he doesn't know where he's going.'

'So how do we know which way he went?' asked Sam.

'We don't,' said Mulberry. 'But I bet I know which way he didn't go.'

'Where?'

'The road,' said Mulberry. 'He was terrified yesterday, so he won't be too keen to go near tarmac any time soon. He'll try to get to the stud going across country and there is only one traffic-free ride he has been on since he got here.'

Chapter 14

'**A**re you *sure* he went this way?' asked Sam as Mulberry trotted along the rutted track that connected the fields of Meadow Vale. The wind was getting stronger, and as it swept up from the valley it pushed at them, bending the trees over their heads and screaming through the branches.

'Look, I don't have a telepathic link with him,' said Mulberry. 'And thank goodness, as I reckon his brain cell is lonely. But I know what baby ponies are like. Right now, he's terrified of everything, so he's going to go the route that terrifies him the least.'

'But you're just guessing that,' said Sam.

'Do you have any bright ideas?' said Mulberry. 'Perhaps he's toppled into a feed bin or fallen asleep in the loo? It will only take us an hour to do this route, less if I canter. If he's not here, we can head back to the yard and think of something else. We haven't got much time to find him and there

are plenty of riders out on the road looking for him. We're the only ones on this path.'

Sam sat on Mulberry's back and chewed her lip as Mulberry trotted on at a smart steady pace. Mulberry used to be a driving pony and she put her head down and powered ahead. Her little legs ate up the ground as the countryside whizzed by. But as they got closer to the boundary of Meadow Vale land, there was no sign of Robbie and Sam felt the hope leaking out of her, bit by bit. Fear was taking its place as a bank of black clouds began to build over their heads and the wind screamed louder.

Not loud enough, however, to drown out the sound of cars and lorries rumbling past on the busy road that bordered one side of the Meadow Vale land. Listening to the rush of the traffic get closer made Sam go cold and she squeezed her hands hard on the reins.

'He's not here,' she said, her voice cracking with fear. 'What if he made it out onto the main road? He'll be killed.'

'He won't go near all those cars,' said Mulberry. 'He's not that thick!' But Sam thought Mulberry didn't sound so sure.

'But he might,' said Sam again. 'We took him out on the road through the village, so he might think cars aren't that scary. No one has warned him about main roads!'

'Stop talking about it, Sam!' said Mulberry. 'You're just winding yourself up. We'll find him.'

After twenty-five minutes, they reached the end of the track and came to a huge metal gate that barred their way, high barbed-wire fencing stretching out either side of it. Trees dotted the fence line, and ahead of them was the car park of the local pub and a busy road that led to the town. They had run out of track and Robbie was still missing. Sam's shoulders tightened with fear. Was he on the road? He wouldn't be, surely?

'Come on, Mulberry,' she said. 'We have to check the road and then we will turn back. With a bit of luck he might be back at the yard by now.'

Mulberry planted her feet and refused to move. 'No, he's not.'

'How can you be so sure, when you can't tell where he's gone?'

'Because he's standing right over there in that little copse of trees,' said Mulberry.

Sam looked up and peered into the trees. Sure enough, there was Robbie, still as a statue, his head hanging down to the ground. His beautiful caramel dapples were smeared with mud, while his fairy tale mane and tail were matted and full of twigs. His pretty face, legs, and chest were scratched and bleeding. He was so dirty he was blending into the shadows.

Mulberry trotted over to him and looked down at his legs, horrified.

'What *have* you done to yourself?'

'I couldn't get through,' he said sadly. 'That fence really hurts.'

The muscly little Highland had tried to push through the fence to get off Meadow Vale land, the same way he had pushed his

way through the hedgerow at the back of the field. He hadn't seen the barbed wire that had been blocking his way.

Sam dismounted, unbuckled her body protector, and pulled her jumper off, dabbing at the cuts and trying to wipe away the blood. 'Poor boy! Why don't we go home?' asked Sam. 'Get you cleaned up and give you something to eat? You'll feel so much better.'

'And quickly,' said Mulberry, shuddering as rain began to patter down through the bare branches. 'This weather is getting worse.'

'What were you doing out here?' asked Sam.

'I thought I would practise being out on my own, to see if I could get over my fears by myself,' said Robbie.

'That's daft,' snorted Mulberry. 'No one does it on their own.'

'They don't?' asked Robbie.

'No!' said Mulberry. 'EVERYONE goes with a babysitter the first few times. No one expects you do to this stuff on your own yet.'

Robbie looked at Mulberry with a sly expression. 'So that means you went out with a babysitter when you were my age?'

Mulberry realized what she had just said— and after all the time she had spent insisting that she had never been as bad as Robbie!

If she hadn't been covered in thick black hair, Sam was sure she would have blushed.

'Yes,' she said in a stiff voice. 'I had a babysitter.'

Robbie's eyes gleamed with delight. 'So that means you were scared of the same stuff as me?'

'I never had a problem with cows!' snapped Mulberry.

'You're still a bit funny about rabbits, though,' said Sam.

'They scuttle and you can't see their legs,' Mulberry shuddered. 'It's not natural.'

Robbie sighed. 'This growing-up stuff is hard. I don't think I will ever be as brave as you.'

'It will get easier, Robbie, I promise,' said Mulberry as Sam wiped his face. 'This time next year, you will be amazed at the stuff you know.'

'But I'm so scared!' wailed Robbie. 'I spend all night worrying about the next day and thinking about all the stuff that can go wrong.'

'I used to think like that about riding,' said Sam.

'You *still* think like that about riding,' said Mulberry.

'Then why do you do it?' asked Robbie.

'Because even though I am scared sometimes, I still really like it,' said Sam. 'I would be miserable if I couldn't ride.'

'It's why I kept making myself go out at your age,' said Mulberry. 'Do you really want to stand in a field for the rest of your life?'

'Fields are safe,' said Robbie. 'Nothing goes wrong in the fields.'

'Nothing fun ever happens either,' said Mulberry.

'There is a lot of stuff I never thought I would be able to do,' said Sam. 'Like going showjumping or galloping across fields. I can do it with Mulberry, though.'

'She's still no good at it, but she is trying,' said Mulberry.

'Mulberry will help you with your nerves, *won't you?*' asked Sam.

Mulberry coughed. 'Yeah, sure, 'course I will.'

'But you tease me all the time,' said Robbie.

'That was a joke!' said Mulberry. 'But if it makes you feel really bad, I'll stop doing it, even though you need to develop a sense of humour.'

'Velvet will help too,' said Sam. 'And me and Mum. We'll all help.'

'Really?' asked Robbie, his face brightening and beginning to look hopeful.

'Really,' said Mulberry. 'You're part of our family now.'

Robbie looked at Mulberry. 'Are you going to be my auntie?'

'I'm not old enough to be your auntie!' said Mulberry. 'I'll be more like a big sister, not that you are allowed to ever call me that.'

Robbie squealed with delight and trotted over to Mulberry, rubbing his long neck against hers. 'I *miss* having a sister!' he said.

'Get off!' said Mulberry. 'No public displays of affection!' She thought for a second. 'No private ones either. I don't want you dribbling all over me.'

'Can we go home now?' asked Sam. 'Poor Amy is really worried about you.'

'Yes, it must be dinner time. I'm starving,' said Mulberry as they began to walk towards the stables.

Robbie froze and his eyes widened with fear. Mulberry rolled hers. 'What on earth is wrong with him now?'

'Pheasant!' whispered Robbie, although it came out more as a terrified squeak. 'Just in front of us.'

Sure enough, there was a little pheasant crouched in the lane in front of them, trying to make himself look invisible against the bare earth. The little bird stretched its neck and began to get up as they all stared at it.

'It's going to attack, look out!' shouted Robbie as he flung his big body sideways and knocked Mulberry straight into the hedgerow. 'I'll protect you, Sis!'

Sam clapped her hand over her mouth and tried not to laugh as Robbie shook his mane and stamped his hoofs as he tried to scare away the bewildered little bird and Mulberry pulled herself, grumbling, out of the hedge, twigs and leaves snagging her mane.

'Did you *see* what he just did?!' Mulberry spluttered.

'The stories you've been telling, that was bound to happen,' giggled Sam. 'Perhaps you could explain properly this time?'

'You're no fun,' Mulberry said to her. 'Look young 'un, I was only pulling your tail last time. Pheasants are harmless.'

'Really?' asked Robbie, cocking his head and looking suspiciously at the little bird that had flattened itself against the ground again and shut its eyes tight.

'They are far more scared of you than you are of them,' said Mulberry.

'Even if someone has told you that they eat ponies,' said Sam.

'Watch this,' said Mulberry. She marched

up to the pheasant, dropped her nose to it, and snorted a puff of air. The pheasant leapt up in fright and took to the air, wings whirring, splintering the moan of the wind with its grating cry.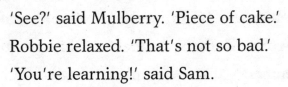

'See?' said Mulberry. 'Piece of cake.'

Robbie relaxed. 'That's not so bad.'

'You're learning!' said Sam.

'Come on, let's go home!' said Robbie. 'I can't wait to see Amy!' He swung his big bum and knocked Mulberry into a tangle of briars before trotting off for home. 'Last one back is a scaredy-cat!'

Sam couldn't help it this time and laughed as Mulberry untangled herself from the briars and shook her mane in temper.

'He did it AGAIN!' squealed Mulberry. 'That's going to mark my coat for ages!'

'Oh, Mulberry, he doesn't know how strong he is, that's all! At least he's developing a sense of humour,' giggled Sam.

Robbie started to sing 'Twinkle, twinkle, little star' at the top of his voice, and the tuneless notes were snatched up by the wind. It was a song the riding instructors used to help nervous riders relax—Robbie had obviously been listening to the lessons. Sam and Mulberry watched him go for a minute.

'You know, Highlands can be a real pain if they are too confident,' said Mulberry. 'They start chucking their weight around and thinking they own the place.'

'He should fit right in with you then, shouldn't he?' said Sam. 'Big sister.'

'Oi!' said Mulberry as they walked after Robbie. 'You can't call me that either.'

Sam laughed. 'You'll get used to it.' She gathered up the reins, put her foot in the stirrup, and swung her leg over Mulberry's back. She clicked her tongue and the two of them trotted after Robbie in the failing light, the pheasant's grating cries shredding through the air, and the wind pushing at their backs.

MEET THE PONIES!

Mulberry

BREED: Exmoor X Welsh. Both Welsh and Exmoor ponies are native British breeds. Both breeds are renowned for being intelligent, which Mulberry definitely is—and she knows it, too! Welsh ponies are often very spirited and lively, like Mulberry, whereas Exmoor ponies tend to have kinder and gentler temperaments. Both breeds are very strong despite their small size, and are tough enough to live outside all year round.

HEIGHT: 12.2hh (a 'hand' is 4 inches. So Mulberry is 12 and a half hands high.)

COLOUR: Jet black   **MARKINGS:** None

FAVOURITE FOOD: Pony nuts and fresh green apples.

LIKES: Sam, going fast, and being the centre of attention.

DISLIKES: Rain, bruised apples, and being told off by Velvet.

Velvet

BREED:

Irish cob. Irish cobs are very sure-footed—making them really safe and comfortable to ride. They're exceptionally kind, very intelligent, and are big and strong, just like Velvet. Perfect for cuddles!

HEIGHT: 15.2hh

COLOUR: Black

MARKINGS: White star in between her eyes that looks like a big diamond.

FAVOURITE FOOD: Any treats, but especially carrots.

LIKES: Hugs, hay, and being taken out for rides.

DISLIKES: Naughty little ponies.

Apricot

BREED: Miniature Shetland pony. Shetland ponies originally come from the Shetland Islands in the very north of Scotland, although they're now found all over the world. Although they're the smallest native British breed, they're also the strongest (for their size). They are really brave, and tend to have very strong characters—which explains Apricot's feisty personality!

HEIGHT: 9hh

COLOUR: Dun with flaxen mane and tail. Dun is a warm shade of brown—like the colour of an apricot, and having a flaxen mane and tail is like having blonde hair.

MARKINGS: None

FAVOURITE FOOD: Hay, and lots of it!

LIKES: Making mischief and getting away with it!

DISLIKES: When Basil comes too close to the fence.

Word Search

Can you find the hidden words listed below?

M	Q	W	B	S	A	M	V	Y	X
U	E	K	C	I	P	F	O	O	H
L	X	A	P	R	I	C	O	T	I
B	N	G	D	J	K	X	H	Q	G
E	Y	U	Q	O	Z	T	R	M	H
R	P	A	F	S	W	C	B	Y	L
R	M	X	V	E	L	V	E	T	A
Y	I	M	H	A	K	Z	A	X	N
E	L	D	D	A	S	M	Q	L	D
C	S	H	Z	R	O	B	B	I	E

MULBERRY

APRICOT

VELVET

ROBBIE

SAM

AMY

SADDLE

MEADOW VALE

HIGHLAND

HOOF PICK

Maze

Can you help Mulberry get to the trophy?

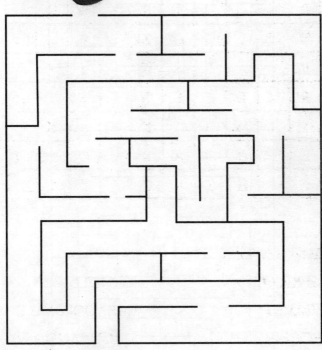

Answers

Word Search

M	Q	W	B	S	A	M	V	Y	X
U	E	K	C	I	P	F	O	O	H
L	X	A	P	R	I	C	O	T	I
B	N	G	D	J	K	X	H	Q	G
E	Y	U	Q	O	Z	T	R	M	H
R	P	A	F	S	W	C	B	Y	L
R	M	X	V	E	L	V	E	T	A
Y	I	M	H	A	K	Z	A	X	N
E	L	D	D	A	S	M	Q	L	D
C	S	H	Z	R	O	B	B	I	E

Maze

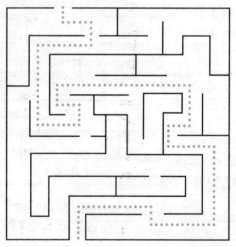

© Lou Abercrombie from Abercrombie Photography

ABOUT THE AUTHOR!

CHE GOLDEN is a graduate of the Masters course in Creative Writing for Young People at Bath Spa University. *The Meadow Vale Ponies* series are her first books for Oxford University Press.

Che's first horse was Velvet, a huge, black Irish cob who not only taught Che how to ride, but taught her two little girls as well. Now, they own Charlie Brown, a rather neurotic New Forest pony, and Robbie, a very laid-back Highland pony. Mulberry is based on a little black mare, Brie, who Che's daughter fell in love with, despite the fact that Brie managed to terrorize a yard of fifty horses and vets wanted danger money to go anywhere near her.

Che also has two pet ferrets, Mike and Mindy, and a Manchester terrier called Beau Nash.

Have you read
M★LBERRY'S
other adventures?

Available now
from all good bookshops and online.